T0160960

RITUALS OF RESTLESSNESS

Phoneme Media
P.O. Box 411272
Los Angeles, CA 90041

First Edition, 2016

ISBN: 978-1-939419-82-8

This book is distributed by Publishers Group West

Cover art by E.E. McCollum
Cover design and typesetting by Jaya Nicely

Printed in the United States of America

Phoneme Media is a nonprofit media company, a fiscally
sponsored projected of Pen Center USA, dedicated to increasing cross-cultural
understanding, connecting people and ideas through the art of translation.

http://phoneme.media
http://cityofasylumpittsburgh.org

Book #1 in Phoneme Media's City of Asylum Imprint

YAGHOUB YADALI

RITUALS OF RESTLESSNESS

TRANSLATED BY SARA KHALILI

PART I
PRESENCE AND ABSENCE

Simple. Engineer Kamran Khosravi would die in a car accident. Easy, done. He finished smoking his cigarette with chilling calm, so that for the first time in all the years he had smoked, he could enjoy lighting one cigarette with another and, without wetting his palate, not taste the foul tang in his mouth.

"Does the smoke bother you?"

He rolled down the car window.

"No, sir." The man's sharp Mongol eyes were darting from side to side, unable to remain fixed on anything. Just like the way he talked, with all those annoying questions.

"Where are we going, sir?"

"We have work to do."

"What kind of work?"

He felt less anxious when he talked. He did not want to stay quiet for even one second. Just to talk, about anything. It did not matter what.

"Were you happy with your pay yesterday?"

"May God offer more blessings."

He had put the thermos on the back seat and the gasoline tank in the trunk. It would not take more than thirty minutes to drive up to the mountain pass. By then it would be four-thirty in the morning. Based on his calculations, it would take him one hour to finish the job, making it five-thirty, and it would still be dark.

"Golshah, are your wife and kids in Afghanistan?"

"They're here, sir."

"How many are you?"

"We're nine. Six children, wife, and her mother."

"You've been busy! God bless your stamina. How old are you?"

"Forty, forty-five, just about."

"Don't you have a birth certificate?"

"I did. Our house collapsed when the planes bombed the city. It got buried in the rubble. I searched a lot, but I didn't find it."

"You weren't home during the bombing? Where were your kids?"

"I wasn't home. Three of my children died, along with my wife."

"So this is your second wife? The six kids are hers?"

"It's no good for a man to be without a wife. I was lonesome. I saw this woman, with a mother and two children. They were from my hometown, Harat. I thought it would please God, too, if she were not left without a man..."

He laughed out loud, from the bottom of his heart. Golshah turned and stared at him. For a few seconds, he forgot about everything. And then, as though Golshah had suddenly found the courage, he, too, laughed and asked, "What's the work, sir?"

He picked up the telephone to call Fariba, who was sulking and had gone to her father's house in Isfahan. He hesitated. He could not bring himself to dial the number. What did he have to say to her? She had already decided not to go back to that secluded hinterland where, according to her, she had wasted three years of her youth, lonely and isolated. She would not return, even at the price of a divorce and losing the man she still loved. He had only two options: either give in to Fariba's wishes and request a transfer to Isfahan, where he would have to live under her parents' noses, or leave her.

But was his problem the question of where they should live? Or whether they should separate or not? For a long time now, he had stopped caring about what would happen. Whether Fariba would stay or go, whether they would live in a small town or someplace else. He knew that, with or without her, whether they lived in a remote town or in Isfahan or Paris or New York—which Fariba always talked about with envy—none of it would make any difference. What the hell was wrong with him? What was he after? All he knew was that he had to carry out the cold-blooded decision he had made, even at the cost of a human life. He frightened himself. How had he come to this?

He was not in the mood for breakfast. He took a cigarette from the pack that was on the coffee table, lit it, and sank back in the sofa. All he wanted was to just lie there, put his feet up on the table, balance the ashtray on his stomach, puff on his cigarette, and not think about the decision he had made. It was as if there were another Kamran inside him, one who did not want to be so heartless. If only he could just stay there forever, sprawled out and doing nothing. He heard his cell phone ring. He would not have answered it had the number on the screen not been that of the real estate agency.

"Good morning, sir. I'm calling because I have found a buyer. You said you're in a hurry, and I wanted to let you know as soon as possible so that we can arrange to show him the house."

"Is it for cash?"

"Of course, sir, all cash. And it's up to you how much you're willing to lower the price. As I explained yesterday, cash customers are hard to come by, and I can't coax and sweet-talk him until he sees the place. Of course, you understand, sir."

"All right, I should be home this evening around six or seven. If I'm not here, call me and I'll hurry back. The sooner we wrap this up, the better."

"Most certainly, sir. I'm at your service. And don't worry. Even if this one doesn't work out, I will do whatever it takes to turn the house into cash in a matter of days."

He hung up and took a deep breath. If Fariba were there, she would say, *Don't they let up even on holidays?*

Like that Friday when she had come and stood behind him. Which Friday was it? How long ago? Why could he not gauge time? All he could remember was that he did not close the book he was reading; he sat there, motionless. Then he clasped his hands and rested them on the table. He inhaled the pleasant scent of her Nivea deodorant deep into his lungs. He let her playfully run her index finger through his hair until she reached his earlobe. Then with the back of her hand she stroked his bare shoulders until he had goosebumps, and he waited for her to move closer to his left side so that he could deliberately turn and allow his flushed cheek to brush against her nipple.

"Stop it, girl, stop it."

Acting childish was for such times.

"I like it. Leave me alone, it's all mine."

Fariba's breezy laughter and that quiet spring morning moved his hand and lay it over hers. He clasped her hand with the intention of lifting it off his shoulder, but the pressure of her body and the scent of Nivea from her underarms mingled with the smell of the onion he had eaten at dinner. He stopped resisting and let her play with the sparse hair on his chest, stroke the skin under his earlobe with her lips and the tip of her nose, and purr, "Do you like it?"

But that time, she neither ran her finger playfully through his hair, nor did she twiddle with the hair on his chest.

She said, "Kamran."

Whenever she called him Kamran instead of Kami, he knew there was trouble ahead. He closed the book, leaned his elbows on the table, and started drumming his fingers on his head.

"Go ahead, I'm listening."

"I don't like things the way they are."

Something was stuck in his mind. Why could he not turn to her and smile, or even hold her, just like the old days when he would sit her down on his lap and joke around with her and they would pour their hearts out to each other. Just like those Fridays that he could no longer remember.

"Stop it, Kami. Let's go to bed."

"I'm not sleepy right now. I'll be there in half an hour."

"You're not coming? You don't like me?"

"No."

"Don't you love me anymore?"

How could he explain something to someone when he could not quite understand it himself? Especially to Fariba, who absolutely did not like hearing anything that went against her wishes.

———————————

He had spent the entire previous night thinking. He had weighed every aspect of the plan. He had no doubt. He would settle things with the company, request a transfer to Isfahan, and sell the house. And he would ship the furniture and their belongings by truck. He was not going to find a better opportunity than now that Fariba was sulking and had gone away. He had called her and, after an elaborate apology, had pretended to be despondent, pretended that her sullen brooding had turned his world upside down and that he had no choice but to move to Isfahan. Now, all that remained was for him to choose a cliff on the road to Isfahan and to find someone to put behind the wheel of the car instead of himself. Ever since the previous night when the idea had first occurred to him, he had been reviewing it over and over again, and every time he reached this point, his thoughts became muddled and confused. But he quickly checked himself and stopped thinking about the moral aspects of the scheme. He lit another cigarette and turned his gaze to the people worming their way around on the sidewalk.

"Did we have to drive through the city center?" Fariba asked. They were on their way to Isfahan to visit their parents.

He rolled down the window slightly and held his cigarette close to it.

"I have to give the house keys to Kamali. I forgot to do it yesterday."

Day laborers carrying their bundles were roaming around the circle. A group of Afghans had gathered around a double-parked pickup truck, blocking traffic. He tried to pass them on the left. The cars behind him were honking nonstop. The car coming from the opposite direction was trying to make its way through the horde of men, who had now gotten into a scuffle, fighting to climb into the back of the pickup truck. A man who was clearly the owner of the truck was shouting, "Only three men! Get down from there!" He was struggling to drag the men off his vehicle.

"They're such savages," Fariba said.

He wanted to say, *The poor souls are desperate for a bite of bread. Work is scarce.*

Instead, he said, "Is it too warm in the car?"

"No, I'm just restless."

"We'll get there. It won't take long."

He had to brake.

"When are we going to leave this place forever?"

She stressed the word *forever* with an icy, passive tone.

"We'll leave."

Fariba looked at him with the same edgy chill.

"It would be great if we moved to Isfahan," she said.

He wanted to ask, *What will be great?* Without the slightest emphasis on great.

"Yes, it would be great," he said.

He knew that if Fariba weren't feeling so glum, she would have retorted as she had done two days ago: "All you do is talk. Talk, talk, talk." And if he, too, were in the mood, the bickering would start. But they were both sensible enough to not do anything that would ruin their four-day trip. Perhaps he still needed to allow life to move along its normal course. Just as before. Or perhaps his colleague, Kamali, was right and he had completely gone off the deep end. "Man, what are you doing to yourself?" Kamali had said. "You're holed up in that ridiculous, godforsaken camp and spend day and night butting heads with a bunch of peasants and workhands. For what? The hell with professional advancement, the hell even with you! Have you given any thought at all to what Mrs. Fariba must be going through? The poor thing is melting away like a candle."

The phrase "like a candle" was directly related to the looks the two of them had been exchanging. In the beginning, he had taken it all as a good omen, and he was happy for Fariba. He had thought that it would help her adapt to that unfamiliar environment more quickly. And for that reason, he had increased his contact with Kamali, especially since they both worked for the Watershed Management Department. But events had not unfolded the way he had wanted them to, or at least not the way he had expected them to.

A man was rapping on the car window with his knuckles. It was only then that he heard the cars honking behind him. He changed gears and drove on. His eyes were still fixed on the long lines of day laborers. He had to pick an Afghan from among them, an Afghan who was an illegal immigrant, whose being or not being made no difference to anyone. It would be difficult to find a fellow Iranian who had nothing and no one—for instance, a homeless man whom no one would look for if he were to disappear. But there were a lot of illegal Afghans and no one cared about them.

Further on, he again eyed them in the rearview mirror. One of them was about the same height and size as him. He pulled over and climbed out of the car. The men stormed toward him.

"I don't need a worker!" he hollered. His eyes were on the Afghan who had the same build as him. Kamran subtly winked at the man and made him understand that he should discreetly follow him. The Afghan was slightly heavier than him.

"Do you have a residency permit?" he asked.

The man quickly produced a card from his pocket and showed it to him.

"Yes, sir. I'll do any kind of work, and I charge little."

A few others dashed toward him, pleading that he hire them as well. Each man offered to charge less than the next. Kamran looked them over, but none of them physically resembled him. He waved them all away and told the Afghan he had picked that he had changed his mind and did not need a worker after all. He wandered around the circle for a half hour or so until he saw an Afghan of about his size. The man was older, but age did not matter. By the time he was done, no one would know the man was not the same age as him. All they had to have in common was their height and bone structure.

"Do you have a residency permit?" he asked.

"I don't have it with me, sir," the man said. "But I do good work."

"In other words, you don't have one."

"But I'm a hard worker. Pay me half the rate. Can I come?"

The man picked up his bundle.

"What's your name?" Kamran asked.

"Your servant, Golshah."

"You come here every day?"

"Every day. What kind of work do you have, sir?"

After he had made certain that the man suited his needs, he drove straight to the office to arrange for his transfer to occur as soon as possible and then set out on the road to Isfahan to choose the cliff he needed. One corner of his mind was still thinking about the laborers, about Golshah, with whom he had arranged to meet the next day. And he was not surprised that Tajmah, not Fariba, occupied the other corner of his mind.

A few sandbags had been stacked on top of each other like battlefield fortifications. They were flanked by a pair of tall, yellow metal canisters—used artillery or mortar shells—with a flag erected on each of them. There was a banner: "Felicitations to our fellow countrymen on this pride-inspiring week of holy defense." Every year there was a one-week celebration of the war with Iraq, during which kiss-asses, vying for promotions and more overtime pay, would wear their ill-fitting Basiji army uniforms and address each other as "brother" to demonstrate their enduring revolutionary spirit and their readiness for battle should America decide to attack Iran. Right! A firecracker would have them crawling into a hole, much less an attack by America.

"Your obedient servant, sir."

Even though he was feeling less morose than during the past few days, he had to appear particularly cheerful. He was nervous. He could not understand why he had grown increasingly anxious since the day he saw Golshah and the laborers. He focused his mind on the end result of his plan, and it calmed him down. He allowed that sense of temporary peace to flow inside him. He smiled more broadly than usual at the guard who was standing at the door, wearing a Basiji uniform.

"Aren't you going to punch in your card, sir?"

"No, I'm on leave."

His colleagues would associate his cheerfulness with his transfer, and he would be free of their pitiful and relentless curiosity. That day would be such a wonderful day.

As usual, Kamali had pulled his chair up to department director Fotouhi's desk and was weaving a cock-and-bull story about a project that, if implemented, would prove to be a great success for the department and its director, and a rebuke to the Forestry and Range Management units where no one could stand the sight of Fotouhi.

"Well, well, Mr. Khosravi! Delighted to see you." Kamali's Basiji uniform was drooping on him.

Fotouhi shook his hand without getting up. "Congratulations. The director general has approved your transfer. Don't forget the celebratory sweet cakes. What are your plans? What do you want the transfer date to be?"

"Fifteenth of the month."

"Huh, listen to the gentleman!" Fotouhi exclaimed, then turned to Kamali and said, "Didn't I tell you he's sick of us?!" And he laughed. "Haji, you're no stranger. You know all about what's going on in my life. My wife up and left, and now she says she will never set foot in this place again."

"God save us from the female lot. I know what you're going through. We all suffer, but..." He lightheartedly sighed and said, "Trust in God. What he wills shall come about."

With him leaving, Kamali would become the camp manager. But he was certain the man would not spend a single night there. Sima would have his hide. With Kamali not there, Barratpour would take over as the camp's big chief—he would scam and swindle any way he could, and he would ride roughshod over the workers. The hell with them! Why should he feel sorry for others? The only person he worried about was Tajmah. Thinking about her made him wistful. He knew he would go to see her one last time. If he decided not to, if he could stop himself from going to her, he would save his pride in front of an illiterate peasant woman, but he would forever crave the scent of her well-toned, slender body that nervously and with wonder performed acts that he had never even dreamed of and enjoyed them with child-like pleasure. How he reveled in Tajmah's innocent, uninhibited joy.

The first time he saw Tajmah was the day the men stood in line under the beating sun, so that he would select five of them to serve as guards in the pasturelands on nearby mountains, with a monthly salary of three thousand tomans. Making sure the locals did not bring their herds to graze in those meadows was the easiest job anyone could have. That was why the villagers always scrambled for guard duty instead of having to work on the check dams and the stone embankments in the ravines. And that regular gathering of thirty or forty workers from the village had become the place where they slyly settled all sorts of scores, away from the eyes of engineer Kamran Khosravi, manager of the aquifer systems and, to the locals, the personification of wealth itself.

Unlike the first time, he did not look at their faces, wondering how to select five of them, later realizing that the older men with less physical strength were better suited for guard duty. He remembered the day when, in one of the houses across the way, he had seen a young, agile woman step onto the veranda, quickly cross the front yard, pick up something, and go back inside. She had not reemerged as long as he and the men were there. Just that passing glimpse, without having clearly seen her face, which had turned toward him for only an instant, had sown the seeds of temptation in him to try and find out which one of the men was the man of that house. He could not have been elderly. After a simple inquiry, Kamran had learned that it was Ali-Sina, and he had hurried past him standing in line to put matters quickly to rest. Contrary to his usual practice, that time he chose three young men for guard duty. And he sent Ali-Sina, the woman's husband, to the farthest pastureland in the district.

"Sir..."

He was awake when Rahmat quietly and cautiously called him. He did not open his eyes. He wanted to dwell on the dreams he had had and not have to get up and talk to the man who had opened the door with great trepidation after saying a thousand prayers.

"Forgive me, sir."

With his back turned to the door and without moving, he said, "Hmm?"

"They've stolen the mesh wire from the check dam."

He reached down and rubbed between his legs. He had to urinate so badly he thought his bladder would burst. He hugged his knees, gently pressed them to his chest, and cursed the herniated disc in his lower back. He curled up in the fetal position to reduce the curve of his back. If Fariba were there, she would massage him until he relaxed his body, banished all nonsense thoughts from his mind, and, for a while, even if briefly, surrendered to relief and tranquility.

He pulled on his tank top, went to the bathroom, and washed his hands and splashed water on his face. The bristly two-day-old stubble on his chin bothered him. He shaved, got dressed, and headed out of the camp, first glancing over at Ali-Sina's house, which sat alone across the wheat field north of the village. He thought, *The houses in the village all look so similar.* He did not see Tajmah. Rahmat was waiting outside.

"You left the workers there just to come and tell me this?"

"Sir, you ordered me to let you know the next time the mesh wire was stolen."

"Which dam is it?"

"The lower valley."

"But it hasn't even been a week since we finished that one!"

He walked over to the SUV and shouted, "Are we supposed to have a guard keep watch over every single stretch of mesh wire?!"

Rahmat followed him. "It's the tribal people's doing, the ones who just crossed the border. When you go there, you'll see their black tents nearby."

"How do you know they did it? Your own village folk have done no wrong at all, have they? Who was it that destroyed the willow orchards we planted last year? Did the tribes do that, too? Go back and put your mind to keeping an eye on the workers."

He climbed into the car and rolled down the passenger-side window.

"How many loads of rock has the tractor delivered since this morning?"

Rahmat walked back toward the car.

"Six."

"Full loads?"

"Full loads, sir. Thanks a lot! You don't trust me?"

"Sure, I trust you," he said, laughing. "But I would be less worried if Barratpour was supervising. When he gets there, tell him not to record the deliveries on the card until I get there."

Rahmat knotted his eyebrows and said, "Of course, whatever you say, sir. What should I prepare for lunch?"

"Nothing, I'm invited to lunch."

The dust the car raised in the air did not allow him to see Rahmat in the rearview mirror. If he had not slept until noon, he could have gone to the office himself to pick up the day's wages, and Barratpour could have stayed at the construction site to supervise the workers. But he was still savoring Tajmah's afternoon visit from the day before. After lunch, he had sent Rahmat on some fool's errand, and he did not expect Barratpour to return from the site until dusk. Wearing only his shorts and undershirt, he had stood and watched Tajmah wash his clothes. Ali-Sina had agreed for his wife to come twice a week to do his laundry, clean the camp, and get paid a thousand tomans a day. He had waited for her to finish her work and to come and stand in the doorway of the room behind the office—the camp's resting quarters—and say, "Is there anything else you want me to do, sir?" so that he, purposely lying down on the bed, would slowly turn, look at her for a few seconds, and say nothing. Just long enough for the woman to have to repeat, "Is there more work?"

To his surprise, she was not nervous. Although she was not immodest, she had not covered herself all that carefully. Other than the two locks of hair that had neatly, as though carefully lined, escaped her traditional tasseled headscarf, and her arms that were bare up to just above her elbow, it was not clear whether she had intentionally or carelessly allowed the fair skin below her neck, slightly above her breasts, to remain easily visible. And he was not the type of man who would not enjoy such a sight. When he got up to give her the thousand-toman bill, he had stared directly into her dark eyes that quickly looked down. She smelled of soot and milk.

"Today's wages."

Tajmah had taken the bill and crumpled it in her fist.

"When should I come again?"

"Thursday. Come in the afternoon."

He had heard her say "Yes, sir" as she turned to leave, and he had followed the curved outline of her behind as she walked out the door, just like the first time he had seen Fariba. He imagined Fariba dressed in colorful folk clothes, living in an outlying house made of cement blocks. He pictured their future sons and daughters running after her as she carried a block of dried cow manure, she chiding them while breaking the block and throwing the pieces in the fire under the cooking pot.

He was in front of Tajmah's house. He parked a short distance away. Just like all other times, her children crowded around the SUV and started climbing up every side of it. They were no longer cautious like they had been that first time. They seemed to have understood that, no matter what they did, no one would reprimand them.

"What are you cooking, Tajmah? Lunch?"

"Welcome, sir. It's nothing worthy of you."

With the back of her hand, Tajmah rapped the boy playing with the side-view mirror on the scruff of his neck. "Don't touch that, child. It's not a toy."

All he could see of her timidity the day before was the faint blush on her cheeks.

"Please come in, sir."

"Ali-Sina hasn't come back yet?"

"He's not coming for lunch."

"So whose lunch is in that pot?"

She smacked the boy again, grabbed him by the arm, and dragged him away from the car.

"It's bilhar leaves. For pickling."

"You're boiling them?"

Tajmah covered her mouth with her hand and giggled. "For its bitterness to come out. I'll put a bowl aside for you."

He did not want to lose the opportunity. He took three one-thousand–toman bills from his wallet and held them out to her.

"Here, for the pickle. I'll pick it up on my way back."

She would not take the money. He gave it to one of the boys and left.

As he drove up the snaking road along the mountain pass, he thought it would not be madness at all to drive with his eyes closed and put himself in the hands of fate, which in the past few years he had foolishly come to believe in. To him, a better rationalization for the conduct of lazy people had still not been conceived. He was almost at the highest point of the pass when his cell phone rang.

"My shitty luck," he said out loud.

His phone had no reception anywhere in the area, but he had not considered the high altitude of the pass. He glanced at the screen. It was his parents' home number. It could not be his father; he would be at the store at that hour. And his mother was illiterate and could not dial numbers. That left Roya, his sister. If only he had turned off the phone, he could have come up with some excuse later.

"Hello?"

It was his mother. Roya must have dialed for her.

"Hi, Mom. How are you?"

"I'm well. Why don't you answer your phone? Where are you?"

"I'm on the road, Mom."

"Your dad called many times last night and you weren't there."

"I was invited to a colleague's house. I forgot to take my cell phone with me. And by the time I came back, it was late and I didn't want to wake you up."

"With the situation you're in, this is no time for you to be going to parties!"

"It was the department director, Mom. Everyone from the office was there. It wouldn't have been proper for me to not go. He just returned from a pilgrimage to Mecca. We had to pay him a visit."

"May we be so blessed. I keep telling your father to sign us up so that we can go, too. But every time I mention it, may God forgive him, he blasphemes at the earth and sky."

"God willing, it will work out. I will sign you up for next year, but Dad has to agree to go with you. You can't go alone. Is Roya there?"

"She went to Fariba's house to try and convince her to end this nonsense and get back to her life. That's why your father was calling you last night. Fariba's father, Haji Mansour, has sent word, asking why Kamran doesn't come to make amends and take his wife back home. The gentleman has also been making snide comments that have reached your father's ears. He's been saying that if this and that don't happen, he will demand his daughter's marriage portion. Your dad got so upset that now he's completely ignoring Haji Mansour."

He was now driving down the far side of the pass. He could see the camp from up there. He looked for Tajmah's house. All he saw were a few blurry dots.

"Mom, we're going to get cut off any minute. I'm driving down the pass and I'll have no reception down there." She did not know that, if he wanted to, he could pull over right there and talk to her. "I'll call you tonight. Is there anything else?"

"No, son. Take care of yourself. Do something so that your wife comes back home. People talk. It's not good in the family. Just yesterday, your uncle's wife was here. She made a few sarcastic remarks. So, I just said, 'My daughter-in-law has gone to visit her family.' Kamran, what are you finally going to do?…"

He hung up and pushed down on the gas pedal. After the second bend in the road, he glanced at his cell phone screen. There was no reception; he could not be reached until nighttime. He had forgotten to ask his mother who had dialed the number for her.

A soldier carrying an army duffel bag on his shoulder was walking along the white line in the middle of the road. As soon as he saw Kamran's car, he moved over to the shoulder and raised his hand.

"Hop in."

The soldier put his duffel bag next to his feet and his hat on his knee. He was holding a gift-wrapped box.

"Thanks a lot, sir."

"Where are you stationed?"

"The other side of the world. Urmia. For someone like me, who had never left his hometown, Urmia is the other side of the world. I'm on leave."

"How long have you served?"

"I've done nine months."

He put the gift-wrapped box on the dashboard and shifted his duffel bag. "Are you from the Social Aid Committee?" he asked.

In every village he went to, that was the first question people asked. Rich and poor, everyone was receiving assistance from the Social Aid Committee. Even Kamali, who earned twice as much as he did, would say, "You have to milk the government as much as you can. After all, it's not their father's money, it's ours by right."

The soldier tossed his duffel bag on the back seat and put the gift-wrapped box on his lap.

"A gift?"

The soldier blushed. "It's a Turkish headscarf. For my betrothed."

He was trying to talk like Kamran.

"And I've brought her some sugar-coated almonds, a souvenir from Urmia."

"How long has it been since you last saw her?"

"Six months. When I was leaving the village, I saw how far down the road she followed me and cried." He stretched out his arm and protracted the word *far*.

"How many days' leave do you have?"

"Twelve days. I've been on the road for a day and a half. It took me thirteen hours to get to Isfahan. Last night I missed the ten o'clock bus. I slept at the terminal and left this morning. The bus ride here was six hours. Well, two days of my leave, wasted."

"But it's worth seeing your betrothed, isn't it?"

He laughed. "Sure it is. I would follow her to the end of the world."

When they crossed over the hill, he said, "Here's my village."

The houses were scattered along the hillside, two or three together. At the end of the village, on the valley floor, a river narrowed. When they reached it, the soldier suddenly jolted and said, "Pull over, pull over!... Nari is at the mill."

He was looking at the mill near the river and at the young girl who had walked out carrying a burlap sack. Kamran stopped the car. The soldier got out and flung his duffel bag over his shoulder.

"Thanks a lot," he said. "She's my betrothed." And he ran down to the river, laughing. The girl stopped and looked over.

"Nari! Hey... Nari!"

He rested his hands on the steering wheel and watched the soldier as he reached the girl, put his duffel bag on the ground, and started unwrapping the gift box. Ignoring him, the girl picked up her burlap sack and walked toward the mule tethered to a tree nearby. The soldier held up a headscarf with both hands and said something. The girl put the sack on the mule, walked back, snatched the headscarf from him, and tossed it in the river. The scarf got caught on a branch. The soldier ran after it. Ignoring him, the girl prodded the mule and set off. The soldier was reaching out to grab the headscarf. One corner was playfully floating on the water. The soldier swung from the branch and grabbed it. Then he looked back at the girl and shouted something. The girl did not turn even once to look at him.

He got out of the car and walked a few steps down the hill. With his back to the soldier and the girl, he urinated behind a rock and tried to hear its sound, which was being drowned out by the current of the river. If he could hear it, he would remember the most romantic moment of his life, and he could allow a strange and distant longing to drive him to despair. He could not and would not. He closed his zipper and went and sat in the shade of a boulder, facing the valley. He stretched out his legs and, loose and relaxed, did not think about the recent days. He was slowly growing accustomed to the drabness of days that were supposed to be cherry red. According to Fariba, that lack of color was a case of chronic depression that people found sickening, and what she meant by "people" was undoubtedly herself and no one else. How he yearned for a cozy corner where he could lay down his head and sleep. To sleep for so long that he would wake up at the age of eighty, and then, because of having been afflicted with lung cancer due to the excessive use of tobacco products—which he would have certainly used had he been awake—he would again lay down his head and this time die. He tucked away the thought of what Fariba would do during his forty-seven-year sleep in one corner of his mind. He preferred instead to think about absolutely nothing with the other corner, which was filled with all sorts of different Faribas.

Clutching the headscarf, the soldier was running after the girl, who was now near the village. Kamran lit a cigarette, took a deep drag, and did not get up. He sat there until the soldier reached the girl and forced her to stop, so that he could hold up the scarf in front of her. Kamran made a deal with himself: If the girl took the scarf, he would go after Fariba to Isfahan. Otherwise, he would follow through with the decision he had made. How he enjoyed his small, harmless games. He wondered whether he should wish for the girl to take the headscarf or not. He knew the soldier would not be the loser in that game. And it did not make any difference anyway. Even if the soldier lost, he would still have to go after Fariba. Did he have any other choice?

———————————

He went to inspect the two check dams in the ravine. Ever since the previous year, when soil erosion had started to increase in the region, the department had sent orders that the check dams should all be constructed with rocks. They would pile up rocks, enclose them in mesh wire netting, and erect them as a solid wall blocking the path of the erosion. Because the mesh wire was galvanized, some locals were stealing it and reselling it in the bazaar.

There was no sign of the mesh netting. He looked out at the black tents the nomads had set up farther away, near the river. A woman was standing next to a tripod with a large goatskin pouch suspended from it. She was churning butter by rocking the sack back and forth. He walked along the dams, got back into his car, and drove away, ignoring the tribal children who had gotten into a brawl over a bowl of whey.

What was he doing? Where was he going? He was driving and thinking only about Tajmah and the excuse he had to concoct to go to her. What troubled him was not the thought of Fariba or the presence of the villagers; it was finding a way to get rid of Tajmah's children. The solution he found was to simply leave the car doors open.

"I don't want to disturb you, Tajmah," he said.

He pretended he was in a hurry and watched as the children stormed the SUV.

"Leave them alone. They're just kids, let them play."

The children's distraction coincided with him going inside and the lunch that he did not allow Tajmah to prepare.

"A cup of tea would be enough."

He looked at the white walls and the wooden beams on the ceiling. The bareness of the room bothered him. He knew that just then, Fariba was either laying siege to the wretched house armed with a rag and a broom, or she was on the phone with Sima, griping about the fact that he had not gone to see her last night and that a thousand thoughts had gone through her mind, worried that something terrible might have happened to her dear Kamran.

"Please, sir, here's the tea."

He looked directly into her eyes that, unlike the day before, were not glued to the floor.

"How old are you, Tajmah?"

She laughed and blushed even more. She looked down at the jajim rug, but quickly looked up again.

"What can I say, sir? I don't know. I don't have a birth certificate."

"But, why?"

She shrugged and giggled.

"Please, drink your tea, it's no good cold."

He could not believe that a girl that lively and radiant, who was at most seventeen or eighteen, had several children.

"How many children do you have?"

"Two boys, one girl."

"May God keep them for you. Was your wage enough yesterday?"

"Yes, it's more than I deserve."

"Did you give it to Ali-Sina or did you keep it?"

"I gave it to Ali-Sina."

"Didn't he say it wasn't enough?"

"No, why wouldn't it be enough? He shouldn't dare say a word."

She pushed the tea tray closer to him.

Kamran laughed. "You've got a pretty sharp tongue today. Yesterday you wouldn't even look at me."

He wanted Tajmah to keep laughing so that he could look at the row of white teeth against the background of her olive skin.

"Don't cover your mouth. Do you feel shy in front of me?"

He did not give her a chance to react. He grabbed her hand and said, "Let me see you laugh."

He tickled her as much as he could, delighting in her peals of laughter and ignoring the sound of one of the children screaming. Tajmah interrupted his amusement and said, "Stop, what if one of the children..." And she glanced over at the door.

He got up, turned the lock on the door and went back and sat next to her, and again smelled the scent of soot and milk.

"When did you buy this dress?"

Tajmah gathered her skirt and tried to cover her chest. He took her hand. "Would you like me to buy dresses for you? And a gold necklace?"

She looked up and laughed shyly. "Ali-Sina says it's expensive."

He kissed the back of her hand. "I will buy them for you."

He could not understand why he suddenly thought of Fariba's bra, which he always had trouble unhooking.

The tea tray remained untouched on the jajim rug.

He did not recognize the SUV as he drove into the camp. Rahmat was outside washing his own clothes.

"Rahmat, who's here?"

"He didn't say. He's been waiting for you for an hour."

He climbed out of the car.

"What do we have for lunch?"

Rahmat abandoned his clothes and got up.

"Sir, you told me not to prepare anything."

"Kill a chicken and roast it."

He burst into laughter when he walked inside and saw Kamali. "You should have called ahead. We would have slaughtered a camel to celebrate! What brings you around?"

Kamali said nothing. He did not look at him either. He was fiddling with the chipped edge of the desk. Kamran sat down next to him. He was thinking about the refreshing hour he had spent with Tajmah.

"Has something happened?"

"What do you think?" Kamali said as he got up.

He did not want to ruin the lingering pleasure of the carefree time he had spent. He thought he could preserve it until that evening or even the next day. It was Thursday and Tajmah would be coming again to do his laundry.

"Come on," Kamali said. "Let's get going."

He held the edge of the desk and pulled himself up. "Where to?"

Kamali turned and stood facing him. "Being supposedly so decent, you should have at least called her and told her you would not be going there last night."

Trying not to lose his temper, he chuckled and said, "Why are you angry? Did Fariba say something to Sima?"

"You really are infuriating when you behave like a louse."

He took note of Kamali's uncharacteristic seriousness and stopped laughing. He walked over to the window and looked out at Rahmat, who was gutting a chicken.

"I swear, I'm embarrassed to have to even say anything," Kamali said. "Do I have to come and tell you that your wife is alone and abandoned? Imagine how much she has suffered that she sent me to fetch you."

He said *me* so loudly and with such weight that Rahmat stopped for a moment and turned to the window.

"My good man, a little common sense…" He huffed. "Don't you feel any sympathy for the woman you dragged to this strange place and left alone at home two or three nights a week? I swear…" He didn't finish his sentence.

He wished he could turn around and tell Kamali that he knew why someone like him was now feeling sorry for someone like Fariba. He was disgusted by all the things he wanted to say.

Kamali sighed and headed for the door.

"You're never going to learn."

"Won't you stay for lunch?"

"What did you do with the house?" Kamali asked. "Did you find a buyer?"

"He's supposed to come today."

"You're rushing into this. I don't want to meddle in your affairs, but if you show some patience and wait, you can get more for it. The real estate market is stagnant right now."

"I don't have a choice. The way things stand, I can't live at my father's house, and I can't become a live-in son-in-law. I have to find a place quickly. To rent, I have to have five or six million tomans in hand. And, given the scruples of the people around here, who can I trust enough to accept a check from them? I'll sell for cash. A couple of million cheaper, but with far fewer headaches."

He remembered the day he and Fariba were driving to Isfahan. He had stopped by the office to give the house key to Kamali. Fariba had stayed in the car. He had handed him the key and said, "If I don't make it back on Saturday, write it up as vacation time. And I don't have to give you instructions about watering the plants. You already know how sensitive Fariba is about them."

He did not know how much of his sarcasm Kamali had grasped. He had kissed him on the cheeks and said, "Take care. Is there anything you need from Isfahan, other than nougats, which they will make me bring for you anyway?"

Kamali had forced a laugh. His eyes were probably searching for Fariba. Kamran had intentionally parked behind the building so that the car would not be in view of the front door. Kamali said, "Give my special regards to your father. Tell him I said if he doesn't deem me worthy of a visit, he should at least invite me over for a few lively hands of cards. Ever since the last time, I just don't enjoy playing with anyone else."

He was relieved that Kamali did not offer to walk him out. His cold attitude and Fariba's complaints after their return, when Sima would tell her Kamali's version of events, were worth the man not coming to the car and exchanging secret looks with her, which would ruin their trip. It was surely worth it, even though he was still not certain of anything. Perhaps there was nothing concealed in the occasional glances and jokes they exchanged, perhaps it was only his uncontrollable imagination and misplaced eastern chauvinism that together were ruining a four-year friendship. Even if he were to judge unfairly, excluding work-related disagreements that could happen at any time and with anyone, he had no ill memories of Kamali, other than his occasional grumbling. In fact, it was Kamali who often had to tolerate his nasty temper—a term he himself used to describe his sudden and unprovoked outbursts—and that was no small merit. Much of the acrimony that in recent years had developed between him and his old classmates, relatives, friends, and colleagues was because of this same nasty temper. And in the early days, what fights he and Fariba had had because of his unpredictable and, according to her, horrifying, tantrums. She once said, "When a storm is coming, one can tell from the dark clouds that precede it. But your storms are cloudless and come without warning."

Kamran had immediately retorted, "And rainless, right?"

"Oh, how touchy!"

The more he thought about it, the less he understood why at times like that they always ended up having a fight.

"So I'm a jerk, right?"

"No, you're not. You're just a little weird."

"And is weird good or bad?"

"I would like to say good."

"Meaning it's bad?"

He was looking into those eyes that in bygone days had driven him wild. Was the secret to that unrestrained passion and raging adoration the mysteriousness of dark eyes, or simply the hidden emotions of youth in a man who was scarcely thirty-eight? Could he figure it out?

He stared at the broken white lines in the middle of the road that were dashing by. He loved the solitude of the road, its twists and turns and deep cliffs. They were still far from the Maymand Pass, where Fariba knew they would spend at least half an hour appreciating the peace and splendor of the oak trees that flanked the road and then they would enjoy the small pleasure of their customary morning flask of tea and some bread with butter and cheese.

"I wish we could go there."

She was pointing at the foothills of Dena Mountain.

"If you want, we can even climb Dena."

"Can we?"

She was as excited as a child.

Sima said, "I'll come, too. I have never climbed up to any peak. This is great!"

It was the first time they had come to the mountains with Sima and Kamali, who had been married for less than a year. It was the same year Kamran had driven there straight from the university, and, with no work experience at all, had been hired by the Department of Natural Resources. Two weeks later, Kamali had been transferred there from a small town in the south, and they had hit it off that very first week.

"Only if you can tell me where Dena ranks among the highest peaks in Iran." He glanced over at Kamali.

"Well, Damavand is the highest one," Fariba said.

He clapped. "Bravo to your general knowledge."

"I don't know either," Sima said. "Do you know, Kamali?"

"Some people mistakenly think it is the third highest peak in the country," Kamali said coolly. "Dena has about forty-eight peaks, none of which are among the tallest in Iran. But it is one of the most beautiful and picturesque mountain ranges. Anyone who visits Dena once falls in love with it. Like that Austrian professor who comes here for two or three weeks every year."

This time he clapped louder. "What else could I ask for in this world when I have such an educated and perceptive colleague? Do you know what I would do if I were in Mrs. Sima's place?"

"Of course," Sima said. And she ran over and kissed Kamali on both cheeks. "This one is for being smart, and this one is for our love."

Kamali blushed and pushed her away. Fariba was laughing.

"If only God would give me such luck," Kamran said.

"Don't be childish. He deserved it."

"If I tell you the exact height of each peak on Dena, down to the millimeter, I'm still not likely to get anything in return."

He ran off uphill and Fariba chased after him.

"Stop if you dare and I'll show you."

He climbed up to the boulders, stopped for an instant, and looked back at Fariba, who was panting and trying to catch up with him. He shouted, "Excellent! Good girl, faster."

Fariba stopped. What a day that was. The first day of their honeymoon.

"Kami, I can't. I'm short of breath."

"You can. If you want to, you can."

He put the blanket, the basket, and their gear on the ground. "Rest a little and we'll start again."

The Renault that Haji Mansour had given Fariba as a wedding gift looked like an ant all the way down at the foot of the mountain. Before leaving her parents' house, after they had passed under the Quran, Fariba's mother had cried and said, "Swear on your life and on my Fariba's life that you will be careful."

Three days had passed from their wedding night, which both their mothers had insisted should be arranged based on tradition: The husband and wife would go to the bridal chamber, and Fariba's mother and the women in her family would wait behind the door for them to have sex and for the blood of virginity to stain the white cloth that had been spread on the bed. The bloodstained fabric would be proof of the bride's purity, and her mother would show it to everyone.

Kamran had said, "I would rather die than submit to such a ludicrous ceremony." He had told Fariba,

"This ritual belongs to idiots. Isn't it stupid for you and I to be making love in a room while a bunch of women lurk behind the door, cracking watermelon seeds and giggling until morning, just so that they can see proof of the conquest on a piece of cloth?"

"I don't like it either," Fariba had said. "But my mother insists on it. And your mother wants it, too. They're traditional. What can we do?"

Kamran had not given in, and chaos had ensued. The wedding was about to be called off. Fariba's mother insisted that her daughter was pure and everyone should know it, and she had cited the example of one of their neighbors. The bride's family had been lenient in this regard and, the day after the wedding, the groom and his family had ganged up and demanded a divorce because the girl had not been a virgin. "I don't want my daughter to be ruined," she said. "If someone makes an accusation tomorrow, what proof will we have to offer?"

It was disgusting. Many—especially city people—no longer observed such old-fashioned customs, but Fariba's family was adamant. The squabble got worse. Kamran on one side, their families on the other. And Fariba stuck in the middle. She did not want to hurt her mother or her future husband. In the end, the elders of the two families had intervened and found a happy medium: The bride and groom would go to the bridal chamber as planned, but they could dispense with the bloody sheet.

That was the worst night of Kamran's life. The bridal chamber, adorned with colorful lace and crepe paper, was a room on the top floor of his parents' house. Fariba had put her arms around him and kissed his lips. "My darling, forget about them. I don't want to see you upset, especially not on the first night of our marriage. Smile!"

Kamran had smiled, just to please her. And then he had lay down on the bed with his back to her and pretended to be asleep.

"Was it my fault?" Fariba had asked.

"You didn't back me up. You didn't try hard enough."

Until dawn, they lay awake with their backs turned to each other. The next day, there were more festivities and the patakhti ceremony, during which the families of the bride and groom offered them their gifts. Fariba had said, "I swear, this is the last one. After the patakhti everyone will leave and it will be just us, you and me."

They did not make love during the three days they stayed at her father's house. Fariba was upset, and now she, too, was not speaking to Kamran. They were both being obstinate, but they kept up appearances so that no one would suspect there was trouble between them. When they were saying their good-byes, despite all their efforts, Fariba's face was awash with unhappiness. Everyone, especially his family, attributed this to her sadness over leaving her parents' home and did not pester them about it. But that same day, Kamran had a thought. He had to do something to catch her off guard.

He could right then tell Fariba, who was being difficult, everything. But he did not. In fact, he intentionally did not speak at all during the entire drive. She did not say anything either. She was sulking and staring out the car window.

"Are you upset?"

He had to draw her out gently. It would take only an hour for them to reach the Maymand Pass, the place where he wanted to execute his plan.

"I know you're angry with me."

He thought he might be running out of time and should have perhaps started sooner. He suddenly burst into loud, roaring laughter. Fariba turned and glanced at him. That was just the opportunity he needed.

"I have a surprise for you, a really big surprise that you will not forget as long as you live."

He knew he had piqued her curiosity. Now it was time to remain quiet. He had to wait for her. A small spark was all he needed.

"I have to share something with you that I have never…"

That was enough. Like a hunter who knows that his prey has fallen into the trap and who saunters toward it while imagining himself savoring a delicious kebab, he patiently and eagerly allowed Fariba to thrash about in dread and confusion all the way up to the Maymand Pass.

He pulled over on the dirt shoulder, parked under an enormous oak tree, and climbed out of the car.

"And here's the pass you always wanted to see."

From up there the winding road looked like a snake.

"Just like a coiling snake… hisssss… isn't it beautiful?" With his hands he imitated a slithering snake. "Eating the first official lunch of our life together in the foothills of Dena will be great, won't it?"

The hissing sound made Fariba scream and dash toward the car. He hurried over to her.

"What happened, my sissy little lady?"

Fariba pointed at the ground, unable to speak.

"It was nothing." With his foot he raked through the dry leaves and twigs. "See… there's nothing." He took her hand and pulled her to himself.

"It looked like a giant lizard."

"It must have been a chameleon. They're harmless. You say boo and they scurry away."

Fariba's face was as white as chalk. He filled a glass from the Coleman water cooler and gave it to her.

"Drink this, you'll feel better. It ran away scared of you and you of it."

Without expecting a response, he started unloading their gear from the car piece by piece. "This is a protected area. No one can hunt here. There are a lot of wild goats and mountain goats. And you can find plenty of snails, turtles, and chameleons." He made no mention of snakes and boars. He handed her the thermos of tea and took the blanket, the basket, and the water cooler.

"Enough resting. Let's go."

"It's fine right here, Kami. I'm begging you."

"You mean you are that shaken up?"

"I'm scared. It's creepy. There's no one here."

"This is the old road. No cars, no people. Just us, all alone."

He continued to walk uphill.

"And the surprise has yet to come."

"Kami, I'm afraid. I'm not climbing up."

"What do you mean you're not climbing up?"

"I won't. Let's just sit here."

From where he stood, he silently looked down at her. After a moment, he said, "You want to sit right there? Are you sure?"

He did not allow the delightful storm inside him to reveal itself in the tone of his voice. Fariba, as if having sensed that something was about to happen, was standing there, frozen and speechless. He laughed and said, "Remember, you asked for it."

He did not even look around. He tossed their gear to the side, walked over to her, dragged her behind a low boulder, lay her down on the ground, and with one swift move yanked the edge of her white overcoat without looking into her gaping eyes.

Neither one of them heard the sound of the torn-off buttons hitting the rocks.

It was not a bad location. Its only problem was that the cliff was not deep enough and the turn in the road not sharp enough. He got back into the car and again eyed the length of the road. Perhaps he could find a better spot. He memorized the number on the odometer: twenty-four. He did not want to think about the Maymand Pass. He did not even like to be in its vicinity. He drove off and allowed his thoughts to randomly drift through the scum and sewage of the past few years, hoping that it would suppress the temptation to uselessly ask himself the "why" of what he was planning to do. Could he? Was it possible? He slowly filled his lungs with air and, little by little, with utter frugality, exhaled through his nose. He was untroubled by his disregard for the immorality of his plan and his apathy toward Fariba and Golshah, a man he did not know and would kill for no reason. In fact, he easily ignored these sentiments, so easily that he was starting to think of himself as one of the most cold-blooded creatures on the planet, and one of the most laughable. If at that very moment someone demanded to know what had driven him to the point of wanting to kill a man and pass him off as himself—even calling him a "man" and not a "human being," and nevermind Fariba's inno-cence—what explanation could he offer? Should he consider himself a selfish creature? Did selfishness have no bounds? For a moment, he imagined himself a boar, a boar with no emotions and no mercy. He immediately rejected that idea. Perhaps he was not kind, but he was not a boar either. Boars traveled in packs. They liked to ravage everything in their path, and, because they could not turn their short necks, they attacked head-on. The more he thought about it, the more certain he became that he had neither attacked anyone head-on, nor had he destroyed any-thing or been a member of a pack. Then why should he consider himself a boar? No, whatever he was, no matter how cruel and heartless, he could not pos-sibly be a boar.

He looked at his red, puffy, expressionless eyes in the rearview mirror, the result of several days of sleeplessness. He ignored them and tried not to ruin his cheerful mood. Although it was not difficult for him to conclude that there was nothing so important or dear in his world that he would regret losing it, it was hard to act accordingly. He had to allow his instinctive, innate nature to do as it pleased, even if it was immoral. He could not remember having ever read anything about the connection between destiny and morality. At that moment, all he wanted was to find a cliff that would serve his purpose. That was all. If he could find one where the old road and the new road ran close to each other, he could walk to the new road after he was done and hitch a ride from a passing car. Then the only thing left would be to find a plausible excuse for being there at that hour of the morning. And that did not seem to be too big a problem, given all the other problems in his absurd life.

———————————

"Problems" was not a complicated concept, but engineer Kamran Khosravi sometimes found even actions such as sleeping to be a problem. There was a time when he could sleep for ten or twelve hours without once waking up, but that was back when he was in high school. Those days, girls pranced and paraded around in his dreams, not like in recent years when even in his waking hours he barely had the interest to so much as be intimate with his own wife. What was he thinking? Be intimate with his wife? Fariba? What difference did it make? If not Fariba, then someone else. According to Fotouhi, all women were alike and one could summarize them in two words: pretense and indulgence. Based on Fotouhi's not-so-polite theory, jewelry, clothes, and makeup epitomized pretense, and indulgence referred to activities such as eating and fucking. In the humble setting of the office, the debates about indulgence, particularly among him, Fotouhi, Kamali, and a couple of colleagues, seemed endless, because Kamali (the constant objector) believed that many men possessed that same quality. So much so that their insatiability became disgusting and embarrassing.

Despite all this, when thinking about the concept of "problems," Kamran could not disregard one factor: expectations. Twelve trivial letters. Twelve trivial letters that appeared exactly at moments when he tried to briefly escape the world of small and large problems by engaging in simple activities such as reading, watching a film or napping. The latter, in particular, triggered many problems when Fariba, invoking the twelve trivial letters without openly suggesting anything, would come to him and say, "Do you feel up to going over to Sima's place?"

When visiting Sima coincided with him reading about prehistoric times and the evolution of the Peking man and Cro-Magnons into Neanderthals, what could he do other than close his book, mutter a few useless, clichéd objections, and go visit Sima and Kamali. In the beginning, he believed he had to participate in Fariba's indisputably critical events, such as attending the funeral of the maternal cousin of her paternal cousin's husband, in order to avoid becoming the target of her relatives' minor and major accusations. And he did. He consented to tasks that he could certainly define as problems, until one day when he neither wanted to visit Sima and her husband, nor did he want to go to the funeral of the maternal cousin of her paternal cousin's husband.

With unprecedented resolve, he said, "No."

The silence that floated in the air between them following that exceptional "no" was more fateful than he thought. Fariba had learned to respond to his intense anger with silence. But strangely, surprisingly, she was so flabbergasted that she forgot that remaining quiet would reap a more favorable result.

"Do you have any idea how many hours you have been sitting there, reading?"

"No, I don't."

"It's the weekend! It's Friday."

He either had to resort to doing whatever would silence Fariba, or he had to remain true to his firm "no" and accept the consequences, despite the cautious and conservative side of his personality. It was a game he had started—although the game of marrying Fariba had also started deliberately—and the first rule of a game becoming a game was to remain resolute.

"I choose the second option."

That day, for the first time, they fought like a lowly, foul-mouthed couple, to such an extent that the next day Fariba unexpectedly left for her father's house in Isfahan with a large bag. It was shortly before their three-year anniversary.

He was still squeezing the small rock in his fist. He did not want to look at it. He was astounded when he realized that the only thing he wanted to keep for himself and not ship to Isfahan was that rock. Why? Affection for Fariba? Or nostalgia over a memory that was now meaningless to him?

He had no doubts. When he was waiting for something to happen, nothing would. And when he was not expecting anything, had not planned for anything, everything came pouring from the earth and sky. It was always like that. The surprise he had planned, for them to have the first official lunch of their life together at the foothills of Dena Mountain and for the occasion to be the first time they made love—something that during their engagement Fariba had repeatedly hinted at or outright suggested and despite all her tiff and tizzy he had not given in to, only because he wanted that glorious moment when he would see gratefulness in her eyes—had suddenly and because of one insane, inexplicable act resulted in nothing but a horrified look on her face. Those days—how far away three years ago seemed—he still had the patience and the ability to face the greatest disasters with the simplest reactions. Ignoring Fariba, who was crying and pulling herself back together behind a boulder, he had caught sight of a few drops of her virgin's blood on a small rock. He had picked it up and wrapped it in a handkerchief, confident that a few days later, after she had recovered and the two of them had had a good laugh over that madness, he would show it to her and enjoy her unpredictable reaction. But he had not done that. He had waited for their one-year anniversary to put the small rock—gift-wrapped in a large box with the note "The world's most sentimental anniversary gift, for you, my Fariba"—on the dining room table. And then, with the coldest, most detached tone he had said, "Fariba, your gift."

Recalling the rest of that evening gave him no pleasure. His thoughts had gone too far remembering even that much. He did not change his mind. He did not want to look at the stone one last time. With all his might, he hurled it over the cliff and watched it plunge into the river, just like the thousands of other stones people casually picked up and just as casually tossed in a river or off a cliff for no reason other than lighthearted fun.

He did not know why he had chosen to throw the stone off the cliff where he was going to die in a car accident. He was angry with himself for that trite and pitiful exhibition. Again and again, he wondered whether it would not be easier were he to just get in the car and really commit suicide. Was his inability to bravely and admirably (terms he used when someone else committed suicide) carry out a decision he had logically and rationally arrived at hundreds of times rooted in false fear or in the cowardice of an inferior creature? Or, was it because of his love of worldly things that he pretended to loathe?

Hassanpour whispered in his ear, "Whatever I manage to get above thirty-five, I keep?" And he grabbed him by the arm, dragged him into the agency, turned to the man waiting there, and said, "My esteemed Haji, I told you, the house is new and in the most desirable part of town. You can search as much as you like, but you won't find a nicer, cleaner, and better-priced house. Sir, I swear on my child's life that at this time of the holy month I would never take a single toman unfairly." He turned to his errand boy and snapped, "Bring tea." Then he looked at Kamran and winked. He was stalling quoting a price.

Kamran would have been satisfied with thirty-four or even thirty-three in cash. However, after two days of stringing him along, when Hassanpour offered to buy the house himself for thirty-four and wrap up the deal, he did not agree. He would not take less than thirty-seven. If that shark was willing to pay thirty-four, the house was certainly worth more.

"Look, I did say I'm in a hurry, but I didn't say I am willing to diddle away my property."

His testiness and inflexibility, coupled with the feigned sour expression on his face, would erase any possible suspicions Hassanpour could have about his sudden decision to sell the house and his unusual haste in the matter. Hassanpour laughed and said, "Don't get all fired up, sir. There's nothing to get upset about. We'll sit and talk and come to an agreement." And he laughed some more, and louder, to pacify him. As they made their way to the agency, he allowed Hassanpour to carry on as much as he wanted, trying in his own way to soften him up.

It was thanks to that convenient half-quarrel that a few minutes later a man dressed in a freshly pressed suit showed up. His beard had grown white here and there, and he was holding a string of prayer beads. Hassanpour claimed that the man was a professor at the medical sciences university, had recently been transferred there, and was looking for a nice and suitable home.

"It so happens, Mr. Kamran, that this gentleman is in a hurry, too. It's a perfect match."

Laughing, Hassanpour turned to the professor for corroboration, but the professor only said, "If it is so blessed." Blessed, a word that was constantly on the lips of government cogs and the religious lot.

Those few words told Hassanpour all he needed to know about the man, and he immediately changed his street-smart tone. "God willing, Haji, God willing."

From that moment on, the professor became a haji. Hassanpour took him to see the house and he seemed to like it, but he did not let on. All that remained was the sweet talk, a term Hassanpour used often. The haji professor just listened, nodded every now and then, and said, "God willing."

Kamran was certain he would not feel sorry for the man being duped. In his own way, the professor was a shrewd shark, too. Just like Fotouhi, the department director, who often played both sides. At the office, Fotouhi acted his part as a haji. Prayer beads in hand, he faked reciting prayers under his breath and fawned over the director general so that he would increase his bonuses, overtime pay, and business trips.

And when it suited him, or when he was boozed up—Kamran had once seen him drunk at Kamali's house—he would spew obscenities at the department and its bosses, and he would not even spare the soil, the forests, and the trees. He would piss at duty and the commitment to preserve the natural resources of his ancestral lands.

Hassanpour again took the deed from him and said, "Haji, see, it's worth forty-two, forty-three easy, by check and payable in installments. But the gentleman is selling for cash, at a much lower price. The poor soul has problems, he has to do it. Otherwise, in this day and age, who would sell a twenty-by-twenty-meter, newly built house in the best part of town for forty? Forget about the house. Just the land is worth a hundred per square meter. Look at it from the other side of the equation. Given the inflation and the country's economic situation, consider how much its value will increase in six months. In a year, it will be up by ten or twelve. Ask any agent in town. As God is my witness, if I had the cash, I would never let this opportunity go by. I would buy the house myself and then take the time to find a buyer. In just two or three weeks, I would make three or four million in profits and I'd go on my way. About one million per week. Who wouldn't want that sort of gain? But I'm short on cash, Haji. You understand? I'm just short on cash."

Hassanpour talked so fast and relentlessly, and with such bluster, that Haji, rapt and captivated, forgot to drink his tea.

"Your tea is getting cold. Please, drink."

Kamran wondered what could possibly be a source of joy in the life of someone like Hassanpour.

Long ago, when he was still a decent human being, he tried to judge others fairly, impartially. But this could be another way of doing it; the only problem was the sheer number of people who opted for this other way—an absolute majority.

Had he not been part of this same majority up until a year or two ago? Had he not spent six years working like a dog to have the things he now scorned? And he had done it with the help of Haji Mansour, his father, small and large loans from different banks, and the likes of Fotouhi—people he had to constantly flatter and praise and never forget to bow to, lest... He had given six of the best years of his life for a house and a car that together were not even worth fifty million tomans. A sum that by the calculation of someone like Hassanpour could be earned in less than six months. Grasping the unfairness or, better put, the absurdity of this was not difficult. It was coming to terms with it that had wrecked his life and driven him to lose himself in, as Kamali put it, "a godforsaken camp" in a rural outpost, all in the hopes that his life would return to the carefree days before Fariba—an innocent creature trapped in the fetid swamp of his life, who, given her traditional upbringing, had no way forward and no way back. What could he do when he knew with every fiber of his being that he could not go on? What was he to do with Fariba and that bitter, nightmarish evening when, drained and exhausted, he had stared at his smiling, ecstatic wife, unable to utter a single word in response to the news that they were having a child? Feigning happiness, while a gentle pain slowly crept up to his temples, was another one of those pretenses that, hard as he tried, he could not describe as anything other than another "problem."

———————————

"She wanted to come tomorrow with her brother, Nakissa, so that she would be here to oversee the workers when they pack up the house. Otherwise, she'll worry. It took a lot to convince her not to come because of the baby. She didn't quiet down until Sima promised to keep an eye on the men."

"That's a woman for you. Sima said Fariba is constantly worried about you. She has asked us to make sure you—her innocent husband—don't have a bad time."

The one thing he was not in the mood for were stinging jibes.

"Stop it, Kamali, I'm not doing well."

"I know."

"Then you're sick!"

He pushed his plate away. He had eaten only a few bites.

"You've lost your appetite?"

"Thank Sima for me. Tell her it was delicious, and… well, you know what to say."

"It's good that you're leaving this place. You'll feel better."

But if it were up to him, he would not exchange that far-flung camp for anywhere else in the world. How he missed the scent of soot and milk and grass.

"Yes," he said.

"We have gotten used to having you two around. Sima was saying she'll never find friends as good as you and Fariba."

He tried not to look into Kamali's eyes. He did not want him to start sharing confidences that only a year ago he would have eagerly listened to and had labeled "the useless, petty bellyaches of two decent, hardworking, helpless hirelings."

"Kamali!"

Kamran smiled at Kamali and said, "Sir, you've been summoned."

"Yes! What is it?"

"I'm no match for this kid. Can you come and take him?"

From where he sat, Kamali just shouted, "Sina, son! Don't bother your mother." Then he lowered his voice and said, "You deserve it." And he made a face, just like a child.

———————————

Kamran threw down his hand of cards and said, "I'll go get the water pipe started."

He took the water pipe's charcoal bowl from the cabinet and went out to the yard. He was looking around and did not want to yell, *Where did you put the charcoal starter this time?* He thought about the child who was no longer just words, who really existed. All on her own, without discussing it with him, Fariba had decided to become pregnant, and yet she claimed it was an accident.

"This is no time to smoke a water pipe! It's the middle of the night."

He did not turn to look at Fariba, nor did he answer her.

"If you look carefully," she said, "you'll see it behind the carton of charcoal."

He had looked there twice and had not seen it. He took a fistful of charcoal and the can of kerosene. Fariba walked over to him. He was not going to give up that easily. He was wondering if there was another way.

"Shall I help you?"

Again, he resorted to the usual game of not speaking when he had no other way of expressing the depth of his anger. A game that if prolonged would result in both of them sulking and ignoring each other for several days.

"You don't believe me?"

He started twirling the charcoal starter in the air, forcing Fariba to step back. Childish spite had become an integral part of their life.

"I'm not saying I didn't want children, you know that, you know I love kids. It was because of you that I didn't want to have any these past two years. Because of the promise I made to you. If I wanted to, I would have found a way to tell you, even if bluntly and directly. I didn't want this, Kami. Believe me. I don't know what happened."

He was thinking about what Fariba had said when suddenly the charcoal starter's chain snapped and it flew off, smashing against the edge of the veranda, and raining half-kindled charcoals down on the yard's stone paving. All he managed to do was duck and shield his head and neck with his arms. Kamali was the first to run outside.

"What happened?"

Fariba screamed. Sima ran out after Sina, grabbed his arm, and dragged him back inside. "Where do you think you're going? Are you blind? Can't you see all that red-hot charcoal on the ground? Do you want to get burned and become a burden to me?"

Weeping, Sina tried to get away from her. Kamali

put on his shoes and hurried over to Kamran, who was checking himself and dusting off the ashes. Fariba had stopped screaming. Panicked, she kept saying, "O God… O God."

Kamran said, "Everything is fine. Nothing happened."

He looked at Fariba and held up his hands. "See! All intact. The starter's chain snapped. It's nothing, don't make a fuss."

"We'll clean it up," Kamali said. "You go inside."

He pointed to Sima, who was holding Sina tight against her. "And take the kid."

"I told myself a hundred times to put a one-piece chain on this thing, God forbid something should happen, and I kept putting it off, day after day. Now look!"

"Mrs. Fariba," Kamali said, "do you have a metal dustpan?"

Fariba's voice was still shaking. "No."

"Then bring a metal tray or something. With a pair of tongs, if it's not too much trouble."

He turned to Kamran who was gathering the chunks of charcoal with his foot.

"Thank God they didn't come down on your head."

Kamran raised his hands to the sky and said, "God, I thank you one million two hundred thousand times."

Kamali looked around to make sure the women were not there. "Do you think you're cute, making a joke out of everything?"

Kamran laughed. "Come on, don't be so tough."

"Don't be so laid-back. I've got my eyes open."

Comments like that puzzled him. Other than booze, Kamali was into everything. He did not discriminate, not even against smoking the heavy stuff. But sometimes in a strange way he would put on the brakes.

He would start praying, but only in the prayer room at work. He would rub his index finger and thumb together and say, "It's my pious deed."

And Kamran would reply, "May God accept your prayers. Sometimes you really stink!"

———————————

The sound of the doorbell did not let him finish his sentence. He got up and gathered the dishes of food that Sima had sent over.

"Are you expecting someone?"

"A possible buyer. He's bringing his wife to see the house. Help me clear the table."

"You go ahead. I'll take care of it."

If Fariba were there, she would have said, I told you a thousand times that the intercom is broken. Fix it. How much work could it possibly be? And he would have rushed out into the yard to save himself from a deluge of complaints.

Kamran could hear Hassanpour behind the door. Like most people in that town, he talked so loud that he could be heard a few houses over. Instinctively, Kamran paused at the door.

"… if you like it, leave the rest up to me. What's important is for the lady to approve… Prices can go up and down, left and right, don't worry…"

He lowered his voice. "… the guy is in a hurry. You didn't hear it from me, but a few of his brother-in-law's checks have bounced, he's bankrupt, the payments on loans this guy guaranteed have been delayed. That's why the bank is after them. To save face, they have to come up with the money by the fifteenth of the month. Yes, sir, it's a question of reputation. It's no small matter."

A woman said, "God willing, by the mercy of the five prophets, their troubles and the troubles of all God's children will be solved."

"From olden days it's been said that you can save neither spilled oil, nor a ruined reputation," Haji Professor said. "God willing, it will work out... what if the gentleman is not home?"

"Haji, I checked with him. He'll be here in a minute."

He was thinking about Hassanpour's drivel as he opened the door.

"Greetings, sir. Yours truly."

He smiled and invited them in. And surrendering to Hassanpour's incessant chatter, he walked them through the entire house.

He did not know how much Hassanpour would manage to squeeze out of the professor, but he was certain he would clinch the deal at more than thirty-nine. If the house were to sell the next day, he would have nothing left to do other than to pack and ship the furnishings, which he could do the following day. That left the most difficult part of the plan, and the closer it loomed, the more he worried that it might fail.

———————

He tried to sleep and not think about anything, not even about Tajmah, the camp, and the small, intimate seclusion he had. He relaxed his muscles, stretched out his arms as much as he could and released them, bent his knees ninety degrees and pressed them to his chest, hoping to ease his backache. He made his ankles crack, something that comforted him and he was in the habit of doing. It was all useless. Because of always sleeping on his side and the pressure it put on his jaw, the subtle toothache for which he had recently been treated had started again. He wished he could sleep on his stomach, but because of the curvature of his back, the doctor had recommended that he should avoid doing that as much as possible. He still remembered the morning he had woken up and could hardly breathe, much less make the slightest move. The discs in his spine had locked and, dreading the sudden stabs of excruciating pain, he had lain there like a statue without the courage or the will to move. Warm compresses and Fariba massaging him had not helped. He had called Kamali and asked him to take the day off and drive him to the hospital. The injection he received had lessened his agony.

He reached back and gently massaged his spine while pressing his knees even tighter against his chest. But he knew he would not be able to sleep even if he were not in pain. He sat up, looked over at the wall clock, and tried to tell the time in the faint light of the street lamps that served as his nightlight. He could not. Carefully, holding his side, he climbed out of bed and, on his way to the kitchen, again glanced at the clock. It was 1:50 a.m.

He wished he had the passion to read, like he'd had in the past. When was the last time he had held a book? He could not remember. He put the water bottle back in its place and went out to the small backyard that served as their storage space. The only time he ever went there was to put away or retrieve those of Fariba's things that were too heavy for her to carry.

He turned on the light and made his way through the odds and ends, until he came to the cartons of books from his university days and from before his marriage. Fariba had asked him many times to have a carpenter build a bookcase for them, and each time he had cut the conversation short by saying, "Okay." He did not know why. All he knew was that he no longer had any interest in those games—an expression he perhaps used just to annoy himself. But now, in the middle of a night of insomnia brought on by something he was and was not aware of, he was again longing for those same games.

He put his hand under a carton whose bottom had given way and dragged it forward. He took out one of the books: *Modern Forestry*. He tossed it back on top of the rest of his university textbooks and went over to another carton. He examined the volumes one by one: *Ancient History, A Comprehensive History of Religion, Modern History of Persia, The French Revolution, Dictionary of Political Terminology, In Service of the Peacock Throne, Lessons in Marxism, Iranovich*. He wanted to laugh. He could not believe he had read all those books. It was as if someone else, a stranger, had bought and read them. They all belonged to a six-month period in his thirty-eight years of life, when, for reasons he no longer remembered, he had become fixated on history, philosophy, and politics. Later, he had become obsessed with film and literature, which he had not immediately abandoned after he got married. *War and Peace, The Brothers Karamazov, The Idiot, The Stranger, Back Pain and Ways to Heal It*... this one he set aside. He skimmed through the rest of the books. There were a few screenplays: *The Godfather, Viridiana, The Phantom of Liberty*, and *Three Colors: Blue*. He sat down right there. If Fariba were there, she would say, Don't sit on the ground, it's cold.

He opened *Blue*'s screenplay to its title page: *To the best brother-in-law in the world, who was a lot cooler two years ago. Nakissa, New Years, 1999.* How disappointed poor Nakissa was, when, all excited, he had walked up to him and said, "It was just released, Kamran. Look!" And he, with the most aloof attitude possible, had replied, "So?"

Nakissa had not said that the screenplay was a gift for him. Later, Fariba had tried to smooth things over. She had made Nakissa write a note on the title page, with the excuse that it would help change the down and dismal mood of the world's best brother-in-law.

He rummaged through the cartons and found a videotape of *Blue*. He went back to the living room and turned on the VCR. Holding the screenplay, he sat down on the sofa and fast-forwarded the film to the scene he was looking for.

"Can't you fast-forward this scene?" Fariba said. "It's boring."

He said nothing and watched the woman who was crying and hurrying down the sidewalk. She ran the back of her hand along the walls for so long that it started to bleed.

"Why is she doing that?" Fariba asked.

He did not look at her and continued watching the woman who was now licking the blood off her hand and walking toward a busy intersection. He pressed the pause button on the remote control to again read the woman's dialogue from the screenplay.

"The poor thing!" Fariba said, and she turned to him and asked, "Would you like some tea?"

"Yes."

He took the remote control and rewound the tape. The woman walked backward, licked the blood off her hand, ran the back of her hand over the rough surface of the wall, went back inside her house, and lay down on the bed next to a man. He pushed the play button. The woman took a deep breath, opened her eyes, lifted her head from the man's arm, and called him a few times. Then, still looking at him, she whispered to herself, "It could have been different, but it wasn't."

The man was still asleep. The woman laid down her head on his bare arm, closed her eyes, and breathed slowly and deeply. The image in the next scene, early morning, showed the woman dressed in jeans and holding a small bag, ready to leave. She put a cup of coffee on the bed, next to the man. The man opened his eyes, but he was still groggy. The woman started to speak.

He looked down at the screenplay and together with the woman murmured the lines of dialogue. "I am grateful to you for what you've done for me. I think you won't miss me. You must have realized by now that there is nothing to miss. I'm like any other woman. I sweat, I cough during the night, and in the early hours of the day I have a toothache. One of my teeth has decayed."

Kamran waited for the woman to again leave the house, run her hand along the wall, and lick off the blood, and for her eyes to fill with tears and, without crying, to hurry toward the busy intersection. Then he stopped the film, closed his eyes, leaned his head back against the sofa, and thought about the woman's emotions. He tried to understand why there was nothing that the woman would miss. He heard Fariba. "Why did you turn it off? What did the woman finally do? Why was she running away from her own home?"

She set the tea tray on the table, took her tea glass, put a lump of candied sugar in it, leaned back into the sofa, and stared at him. And he closed his eyes again.

———————————

The sound of the doorbell jolted him awake. There was static on the screen. He turned off the television and the VCR and glanced at the clock. It was 4:00 a.m. Only then did he remember Nakissa and his 10:00 p.m. ticket. He had told Fariba he would go to the bus terminal to pick him up.

"Who is it?"

He could hear a car with its engine running.

"It's me. Nakissa."

When he opened the door, Nakissa was paying the taxi driver.

"I promised Fariba I would pick you up," he said.

"For God's sake, what is this place? And you've lived here for four years? Fariba did well to leave in a huff. Otherwise, who knows how long you would stay here."

He gripped Nakissa's shoulder and squeezed it. "Doesn't your sister make me suffer enough for you, little twerp, to start chirping like a canary the minute you arrive?"

He shoved him inside and closed the door. "Everyone in your family is nuts. It's hereditary. There's nothing you can do about it."

"Haven't you heard? They've discovered the pattern of the human genome. Now they can fiddle with genes."

"God bless their forefathers!"

Nakissa headed straight for the refrigerator. "Is there anything to eat in this thing? I'm starving."

By the time Kamran had fried a few eggs, Nakissa had delivered everyone's news. He brewed some tea in a thermos, smoked a cigarette, and absent-mindedly listened to Nakissa carry on about how maddeningly happy Fariba was. He said she was not only driving herself crazy, she was driving everyone else crazy, too. And why? Because the divine and darling Kamran had decided to grace them with his presence. Kamran listened, smiled out of habit, and touched his temple to stop an incurable headache from exasperating him. He had to remain composed in front of Nakissa, who was now imitating how he would have to report back to Fariba. "My almighty brother-in-law is well. Couldn't be better. We talked and laughed until we were about to burst. I swear, honest. Whose fault is it that he's batty and scatterbrained? He was sane and healthy when he came to ask for your hand, he was cool. But now, he can put a corpse to shame..." Nakissa was chatting nonstop.

When would he be free of these trying games? He prepared a place for Nakissa to sleep and returned to the kitchen. He did not clear away the dishes. He listened to the flock of sparrows that in the early hours of dawn were singing for the sun to rise. He went out to the yard and sat down on the first step of the veranda. He stared at the leaves of the maple tree in front of the house and listened to the birds, but he was still tired, tired.

"What's the work I have to do, sir?" Golshah asked.

"Have you had breakfast?"

"Truth be told, no."

He reached back, took the basket from the back seat of the car, and put it between them. He took one of the two containers of soft cheese and put it on the dashboard.

"There's bread in the plastic bag."

He turned on the inside light.

"What is this, sir?"

"It's cheese. Open it and eat it with bread."

"What's the hurry? I'll eat later."

"No. There won't be time. I want us to start work as soon as the sun is up."

He glimpsed at the man's darting, blinking eyes. Golshah clumsily tore open the cover of the cheese container. As he took the plastic bag of bread he said, "Won't it mess up the car?"

"Put the plastic bag on your lap and try not to get crumbs on the seat."

"Yes, sir. You're right. Bread is a blessing from God."

"There's also tea. Pour some for yourself if you want."

"Aren't you going to eat, sir?"

"I'll eat later. When you start working, I'll have time to eat."

He felt neither sorry for Fariba, nor for his car, nor even for Golshah who was oblivious to everything. His only regret was never seeing Tajmah again and never again smelling the scent of soot and milk and grass. The day before, on his way to the camp for the last time, he had gone to the bazaar and asked a shopkeeper for his most expensive fabric. He had said, "Enough for a nice, proper folk dress."

"With enough for a pair of culottes as well, it adds up to a hundred forty-thousand tomans," the shopkeeper said, and he stood watching him, waiting. A folk dress required ten times more fabric than a regular dress. That was why it was so expensive.

"Cut it."

He had also bought a gold necklace and had wondered what else he could buy for her. He knew that Tajmah might not be able to tell the difference between real and fake gold, but he was spending the money for his own heart's content. He wanted to lavishly commemorate the best and most peaceful moments he had had in the past few years, even if another part of his mind would ridicule him for it. Did he not have the right to want some time just for himself, free of Fariba and his parents and sister and colleagues and neighbors and everyone else? Without anyone expecting a share of it, in exchange for something they had or had not given him?

He told Tajmah, "I want to put it around your neck myself." And he did not let her touch the necklace.

"You shouldn't have gone to the trouble," she said.

He kissed her lips to stop her from talking. Then he moved from her lips down to her chin and neck. He paused on the hollow of her neck and slowly inched farther down to where the necklace would not sit still.

"I'm leaving, Tajmah."

He stared at her smooth skin. With deep, rapid breaths he inhaled the scent of soot and milk and grass.

"May you travel in health. Where are you going, sir?"

He laughed and looked into those earnest eyes that did not understand how memories could be made nostalgic, so that in times of loneliness one can sigh at their remembrance.

"You mean you won't come to see me any more?"

"No, I won't. Will you miss me?"

She laughed, moved closer to him, and let her body touch his.

"You're a good man."

"You like me?"

"Yes, I do."

"Why?"

She put her index finger on the tip of his nose and played with it; something she had learned from him.

"Because you play with me, you make me laugh. It's so good."

"What about Ali-Sina? Do you like him, too?"

"Well, yes. He's my husband."

"Who else do you like?"

"My children, and that ewe that gives so much milk."

He laughed and took her hand. "So, you like everyone."

"No, not everyone."

He played with the fine downy hair on the small of her back and said, "Which one of them do you like more?"

"More?"

Her finger remained on his nose.

"…well, it would be nice if Ali-Sina played with me. He just does his business and goes to sleep." She pinched his nose.

"Tajmah, will you come away with me? Do you want to?"

"And what would I do with Ali-Sina and the children?"

"I will get your divorce for you."

"What is a divorce?"

Her finger remained on his lips.

"That's why I like you. Because you don't know what a divorce is."

"Can't you just come and play with me like this? And let Ali-Sina stay a guard? And let the children go and eat cookies in your car?"

The children could very well be happy eating sweets and cookies in his car, and Ali-Sina could continue being a watch guard. But how could he explain to slender, lovable, childlike Tajmah, whose only joy was to play with the tip of his nose, with his fingers, lips, and earlobes—a simple game she had been denied—why he could no longer go to see her, to slowly, gently shower her with kisses, to tug on the fine fluff on the small of her back and wait for her broken screams and carefree laughter.

———————————

He did not want to stop by the camp. He did not want to see Barratpour and Rahmat. He had nothing to say to them. He drove to the mountain pass, parked the car at the highest point, and climbed out. He stood facing the cliff and looked down at Ali-Sina's outlying house. A thousand times he had considered the fact that he could change his mind, and each time, overwhelmed by melancholy, he had pushed the thought away, hoping for a later day when he could calmly and carefully weigh everything and then decide. And yet, he knew there was no way back for him, just as he knew he could not stand there forever with a lump in his throat, staring at the cement blocks of a secluded house. He laughed at himself, climbed back into the car, and drove off.

He had promised Sima he would buy fresh river fish for her. Driving to the asphalt road, he looked down the narrow trails and along the river's edge, hoping to see the young fishermen who in the afternoons sold their catch at the main intersection. Two of them were down in the valley. Kamran pulled over and got out. He saw the soldier he had given a ride to a few days earlier. The young man was waist deep in the river and holding up a net, ready to cast it in the water.

"Young man, how are you? Isn't it too late to be fishing? When will you have time to sell them? At sundown?"

He walked to the edge of the water.

"They're not for sale. They're for me."

"Do you have any for sale?"

"Don't shame me. For you, of course I do." He turned to the young boy standing next to their fishing gear. "Boy, hurry up and pick out a few of the large ones for the gentleman and put them on a stick."

The boy broke a thin branch from a young tree by the river, looped one end into a knot, and started spearing the fish through their gills with the other end.

"Let me start a fire for kebab."

"No, thanks. I'm in a hurry. I have to get back."

"But it's not good like this. Please, then, come to my home and honor us by staying for dinner."

Kamran's eyes were on the boy who was nimbly piercing the branch into the gills of the fish and pushing it out through their mouths.

"What happened with your betrothed? Did you give her the scarf?"

The young soldier laughed, looked over at the boy, lowered his voice, and said, "I'll give it to her. By the time my leave is over, I'll give it to her. She's just teasing me."

The boy brought over two branches with seven or eight plump fish on each of them.

"Here you are, sir."

"One is enough."

He returned one of the branches to the boy. The young soldier put down his fishing net and took it from the boy.

"On my life, I'll be hurt if you don't take it."

"But you won't have any left for yourselves."

"One thing God has given plenty of is fish. I'll just cast the net twice more."

He took the second stack of fish and said, "Thanks."

The young man picked up his net and rearranged it.

"Give in to her. Don't let her get away."

The young man laughed and snapped at the boy, "Kid, bring wood, start a fire. Hurry up."

"But I already brought wood!" the boy said.

The young man leaped toward him and shouted, "Bring more, you goat! It's not enough."

The boy ran off toward the trees. The young man laughed and said, "He's my brother. It's no good for him to hear, he'll tell Nari."

"Your betrothed?"

"Yes. Her name is Nari, short for Nargol. She's toying with me, her own cousin. I was away for six months, and she's taken a liking to someone else." He winked. "Tonight or tomorrow, I'm going to throw her down on the ground and get it over with." And he laughed out loud.

Kamran joined in his laughter and said, "Well done!"

———————————

"But this guy is an Afghan," Nakissa said.

The man's Mongol eyes looked squinty. Kamali said, "I've settled it with him. Two hours' work for a thousand five hundred." He turned to the man and said, "Right, Afghan?"

"Yes, sir. I already said yes."

The driver, who had backed up the truck close to the front door, walked into the yard and said, "When are we going to get started, Mr. Kamali? We have to think of the other end as well. If I leave around eleven o'clock, I'll be there by six or seven. It's best that I get there before dark."

The truck driver was one of Kamali's acquaintances.

"It's now seven o'clock," Kamali said. "I promise you'll be on the road by ten. Is that good?"

"Even if I get going at eleven it'll be fine."

In three hours, they packed the house and Nakissa left for Isfahan with the truck. Kamran told Golshah to stay and clean the house while he went to the notary public. As he was leaving, Sima said, "We'll be expecting you tonight, Mr. Kamran. On your way to the camp this afternoon, would you take the trouble to buy some fresh river fish for dinner?"

Kamali laughed. "She's asking you to bring fish because she wants to be certain that it's fresh, and she wants to make sure you won't bail out on her!"

"Your serf and servant," Kamran said laughing. "By all means." Then he turned to Golshah. "I want the entire place to be sparkling clean."

Armed with a broom and a bucket, Golshah headed indoors. "Yes, sir."

By the time he returned from the notary, Golshah had finished cleaning the house. Kamran again sized him up to make sure the man was not too different from him in height and build. He just did not have a large stomach, which was not important.

"How much should I pay you, so that you'll come back tomorrow and do some more work for me?"

"As much as your goodwill sees fit, sir."

He took out his wallet. "Here's a thousand five hundred for packing and loading up the furnishings." He put another two thousand tomans in Golshah's hand and said, "And this is for cleaning the house. Is it enough?"

"May God bless us with bounties."

Golshah was putting the money in his shirt pocket.

Kamran gave him two more bills and said, "And this is prepayment for tomorrow, so that I know you'll come and I won't have to go looking for another worker."

"It's not necessary, sir. I'll come."

His eyes were on the money.

"Keep it."

Golshah stuffed the bills in the same pocket.

"Four o'clock in the morning, Jahad Circle. Will you be there? No delays?"

"Of course, sir. I'll be there for sure. If Golshah says he'll be there, he will be there. Four o'clock in the morning, Jahad Circle. I'll wait next to the booth." As he was changing his clothes and getting ready to leave, he asked, "What kind of work is it, sir?"

That simple question was starting to irritate him.

"Why just half a cup? Fill it up, man. It's halal."

He slowed down the car so that Golshah would not spill his tea. It was his second cup.

"How is the aroma?"

"It's good." He blinked a few times. "I feel a little dizzy."

Golshah put a sugar cube in his mouth, blew on the tea, and took a sip. A small one. Again, he blew on the tea. Kamran had intentionally used the fragrant

Ahmad tea so that its scent would conceal the smell of the sedative. Golshah could not possibly grow suspicious. He was blinking more rapidly. His head was bobbing up and down, and his eyes were glued on the road. He put the half-empty cup on the dashboard.

"What's wrong, Golshah? Should I pull over?"

"It's nothing, sir." He pointed to his head and said, "It feels heavy."

"Didn't you get enough sleep last night?"

"I did. I went to bed early so that I would be on time this morning."

He sounded groggy. He fell asleep before they reached the pass. Kamran grabbed his hand and shook it hard. "Golshah... Golshah..."

When he was five hundred meters away from the cliff he had chosen, he accelerated and suddenly slammed on the brakes to leave tire marks on the asphalt. The back of the car swung from side to side and, a few meters away from the cliff, the car came to a stop on a low incline. He put on the handbrake, got out of the car, and wedged a rock under the front tire. He went over to the passenger side, pulled Golshah out of the car, and laid him down on the ground. He took a set of his own clothes out of a duffel bag in the trunk and put them on Golshah. He stuffed Golshah's clothes in a plastic bag and, together with the container of gasoline, put it next to a boulder. He strapped his watch on Golshah's wrist and positioned him behind the wheel of the car. Then he took off his gold chain that had a charm with Fariba's name engraved on it and put it around Golshah's neck. He left his cell phone on the dashboard. He put his wallet, with his driver's license, registration card, work ID, and other odds and ends in Golshah's pocket. He paused. He looked around. He should not forget anything.

After he had again reviewed every detail, which he had considered a thousand times before, he poured gasoline on Golshah and the seats and emptied the container on the car floor. He started the engine, rolled down the driver's side window, released the handbrake, shifted the gear into neutral, and closed the door. Then he struck a match, took a few steps back, and tossed it into the car. A pyramid of flames licked out of the window and forced him back. He kicked away the rock lodged under the tire. The car slowly rolled forward. He went behind it and started to push. The flames inside the rear windshield did not allow him to see Golshah. When the car, engulfed in flames, was plunging down the cliff, he was standing there, watching. He saw it hit the valley floor. He went back and took the rock he had placed under the front wheel and tossed it to the side to make it look as if it had always been there, just like all the other rocks. Then he put the gasoline container in the same plastic bag as Golshah's clothes. He slung his duffel bag over his shoulder and, carrying the plastic bag, headed up the mountain. He would reach the new road in twenty minutes.

PART II
ON A SINGLE WING

ONE

He did not remember if he had ridden on a public bus in recent years, and watched people just for the sake of watching them, perhaps to see something that would entertain him. The strange emotion stirring inside him allowed him to not feel disdain and contempt toward people. He tried to imagine how he would react if one of those passengers were to suddenly slap him hard across the face.

"Sir, these are all nothing but games."

He did not see whose voice it was coming from a few meters away. He was looking at a young man who had his satchel on his lap and a book full of charts and formulas lying open on top of it, but was busy arguing politics with someone. He could not understand why everyone in the country was forever preoccupied with the government and affairs of state.

"They say we should forget about the possibility of a resignation."

He did not want to hear about politics. As a young man, he had wanted to rub elbows with the political pack. He had mingled with them for a while, but he had soon realized that he was not capable of the same deceit and duplicity. Trying not to knock into anyone with his gym bag, he made his way through the crowd and to the middle of the bus. The body odor of the stout young man standing next to him was too pungent to bear. He turned away and watched two men who were in a heated discussion about the previous night's soccer match. One of them was trying to explain why Manchester United had failed to beat Real Madrid.

He bought a melon, a watermelon, and a few cucumbers from the produce shop near his home. Although he had spent two hours in the swimming pool, he walked home without stopping to rest. He saw an old man with a cane, and a young woman coming from the opposite direction. A few steps away from the building, he decided to challenge himself to a game, to try and open the apartment building's front door before the girl reached it and without putting down his load. A long shot since his keys were in the side pocket of the gym bag. Even though the old man was ahead of the girl, Kamran thought if he were to choose him instead, he would certainly win. He did not like playing games that he knew he would win.

He shifted the plastic bag with the melon and cucumbers to the hand that was holding the watermelon, and used his free hand to pull the gym bag forward and unzip its side pocket. The girl was now ahead of the old man and no more than eight or nine steps away. He had pulled out his key chain and was trying to quickly unlock the door when the watermelon tumbled to the ground and broke in two. Losing that little game did not stop him from smiling. He put down his gym bag and the bag of fruits, leisurely opened the door, picked up the two watermelon piec-es, went inside, and put them on the stairs. Then he went back to fetch the other two bags. The girl was standing in front of the door, watching him. She was dressed in brown from head to toe and wreaked of strong perfume.

"Excuse me," she said. "Do you mind?"

He stepped aside to let her in. As she climbed the stairs, she glanced down at the watermelon halves and, without stopping, continued on her way. The strong smell of her perfume mingled with the horri-ble stench on the ground floor that had been irritating him for several days. If he had instead chosen the old man, he would not have had to rush, he would not have lost the game, and his watermelon would not have broken in two. When he slung his gym bag back over his shoulder, the old man was still a few steps away from the front door. Kamran was struggling to stuff the watermelon into the plastic bag and trying to ignore the smell in the hallway when the door to the apartment on that floor opened and a middle-aged man, fifty or fifty-five, walked out. He was wearing a pressed, barely-clean black suit.

The man stared at him and his watermelon halves for a few seconds and said, "Why is your watermelon broken?"

"I dropped it."

"Are you the new tenant?"

The proprietor, an old woman, had mentioned that her brother lived on the ground floor, that his wife and child had been killed in a bombing during the war, and that he had not been well ever since. And she had pointed to her temple.

"Yes, I am."

The man turned around to lock the door to his apartment.

"How much is your lease for?"

"The lady didn't tell you?"

"That old hag doesn't breathe a word." He put his key back in his pocket and waved his cane in the air. "She conned me out of my share of our inheritance with a forged will. And then, after my house was shelled, she took my land and gave me this place instead." He slammed his cane against the door to his apartment. "She swindled me, sir! Have you ever heard of a sister swindling her own brother?"

"Why didn't you file a complaint against her?"

He smirked. "A complaint? Against who? My own sister? Would you ever do such a thing if you were in my shoes? In this day and age, people don't even understand what the other person is saying... How much did you lease the place for?"

"Ten thousand tomans down payment."

The man shook his head. "You poor thing. She stiffed you, too. She's charging you too much. Hashemzadeh, the guy on the first floor, only pays six thousand tomans, and he still complains. The thug! The university girls were hoodwinked, too. Just like you and me. I like Hashemzadeh, he says whatever nastiness he wants to my sister. And I'm in no shape to give him a whack in the mouth." He leaned forward. He smelled of mothballs. "Do you have a wife and kids?"

Kamran stepped back and shook his head.

The man winked. "So, you're free for the time being. Live it up!" And chuckling, he walked toward the front door.

The old landlady had said, "He's harmless. Don't take anything he says seriously." And then, while going back and forth in the apartment to turn on the lights, she had added, "Doesn't the missus want to see the apartment?"

"My wife has passed away. My daughter lives with me, but I've sent her to the Caspian coast to spend the summer with her grandmother."

"You mean you're single?"

"As I said, my daughter lives with me. She's nine."

The old woman had tried to conceal the wrinkles on her face with heavy makeup. "You know how tough it is for a single man to find a place to rent. With or without kids. There are three university girls sharing the unit on the second floor. How could I rent this apartment to you?"

"Mom, aren't you coming?" It was a woman's voice calling out from the stairway.

The old woman ignored her and went to the kitchen. "Everything is clean and in working order. What guarantee do I have that you won't create a problem with these girls? Single men and women who are not kin are like cotton balls and fire."

"Mom!" A woman of about forty, wearing white gloves and a burgundy coverall, walked in. "Mom, I'm late. I have to pick up Yashar."

The old woman walked out of the kitchen and snapped, "Stop making a ruckus, I'm coming. It's not ten o'clock yet." The younger woman raised her eyebrows and mumbled something under her breath. The landlady turned to him and said, "You see, sir. I'm in a hurry. Please…" And she motioned toward the door. "I have to go. I've got things to do."

When the old woman increased the amount of rent she wanted, he realized that all the fuss and flurry was nothing but a bargaining ploy. After they signed the lease, she asked him to not tell the neighbors that his wife had passed away. If he behaved himself, which he promised he would, after a while everyone would get used to having a single man living in the building.

The apartment was no more than forty-eight square meters. A one-bedroom unit with a fully tiled kitchen and a proper bathroom and separate toilet. He put the cucumbers and the watermelon halves in the refrigerator. He was craving a glass of melon juice, but he remembered he did not have a fruit juicer, not even a grater. On the sheet of paper next to the telephone, he wrote *juicer or grater*. He would have time later to decide which one he should buy. Or perhaps both. One thing he had plenty of these days was time, time to think about anything, including buying a grater, an issue that could not be any less important than the evolution of Cro-Magnons into Neanderthals in the span of history, or the obligation to attend the funeral of a maternal cousin of a paternal cousin's husband. At least for him, at that moment in his life when he had an urgent need for fruit juice, that is how it was.

He cut half of the melon into slices and arranged them on a tray. He went to the living room and sat on the floor with his legs stretched out, put the tray on his lap, and attacked the melon like a tiger, devouring one slice after the other. When he had finished, he burped as he pushed the tray away and wiped his mouth with the back of his hand. He lay down on the carpet, spread out his sticky hands, and considered all the things he could do in absolute freedom, in any manner he liked, in the small realm of a life that was void of ups and downs and that he had gladly chosen. He was surprised by the surge of all the energy inside him. He closed his eyes, contemplated that unfamiliar rush, and became even happier knowing that he did not need to empty his mind, as if it were a trash can, of a whole lot of mundane everyday rubbish. Brimming with a steady stream of joy, he flexed and stretched his body. He shifted from side to side and lay there for so long that he finally fell asleep.

It was dark when he woke up. He turned on the light and saw that a column of ants had laid siege to the melon rinds and were now clambering over one another. He did not touch the tray. He went to the kitchen and noisily splashed water on his face and washed his hands in the sink, where he had left two or three dirty dishes. He enjoyed that small crudeness, a conduct that was forbidden to him before and during his marriage. He dried his face and hands with a bath towel and was not afraid to question whether that behavior was out of spite for parts of his past life or if it really gave him pleasure. To him, it did not make much of a difference.

He went back to the living room, lay down on his stomach next to the tray, anchored his hands under his chin, and decided to spend those moments observing the ants. It was as if it were his first encounter with the tiny creatures. The obsession of comparing the sum with its parts, his constant mind game, elevated the ants to the majesty of the Milky Way and the splendor of billions of galaxies, compared to which the Milky Way was no more than the tip of a needle. The ants' universe stretched from the confines of their nest all the way to the melon rinds. He imagined himself as an ant. At first glance, they all looked so much alike—absolute social equality. He wondered how far he could travel as an ant. As far as the kitchen? The bedroom, where a crumb of cake or a speck of sugar might occasionally be found? Or, if there was no food to be found there, even as far as the neighbor's apartment? Would he, as an ant, be aware of the fact that in the capital city of the Islamic Republic he was savoring the sweetness of a melon rind?

He decided to arrange a banquet for the ants living in the Milky Way. He put a dollop of jam, two small fragments of a sugar cube, and a tip of a teaspoon of hazelnut-flavored chocolate spread next to the rinds on the tray. But in his opinion, that undeniably royal feast was still incomplete. He went back to the kitchen and searched the seams and corners of the cabinets and hunted down two not-so-large cockroaches, so that the ants could dine lavishly on a variety of foods.

He heard a car drive by in the distance. He opened his eyes. He could hear a vague whirr that he could not identify or associate with anything. He leaped up and went over to the window. He looked out at the rays of the sun that had again risen in the sky. Once more, he had slept through the moment of dawn, which he longed to see. His stubbornness about not using an alarm clock, which he had intentionally not purchased, and his determination to trust his body's internal clock had together conspired for him to not wake up in time for the fourth day in a row. The previous night, before going to bed, with meditation music playing in the background, he had relaxed his toes and, limb by limb, had slowly moved up and released his chest, arms, and neck. With his eyes closed and his mind cleared of all other thoughts, he had tried to concentrate on waking up the next morning before the break of light. He had heard that, with this method, he could wake up at any hour he wanted, but only if he could manage to think solely and entirely about rising at that specific time. He remembered that, before falling asleep, the last thing he had thought about with total concentration was a simple question: Do ants sleep?

He opened the bedroom window and sucked the air deep into his lungs. He clasped his hands, swung them from side to side, and grunted in pleasure. He was certain that the next day he would wake up right before dawn and he would go up to the rooftop and wait for eight minutes and twenty seconds—what he remembered from his second-year physics textbook— for the rays of sun to arrive. He had to do this.

He looked at the balcony on the second floor of the brick building across the street. At that hour of the morning, a four- or five-year-old boy was playing with a ball. The boy turned to him for an instant and smiled. He waved at him. The boy continued to play. A few minutes later, a sleepy woman with disheveled hair, who must have been his mother, walked out, said something, and then impatiently took the boy by the arm and dragged him inside. A short while later, someone tossed the ball out onto the balcony. It bounced a few times, rolled into a corner, and stopped. There was no sign of the boy.

On his way to the bathroom, he glanced at the banquet tray that the ants had still not abandoned. He did not intend to take it away. He quickly brushed his teeth and washed his hands and face. He ran his hand over his ridiculous beard, which he had grown only as a matter of precaution. He felt gas drifting through his intestines. He stood with his legs slightly apart and pushed, but he did not hear anything other than a small sound, a *pfft*. He made faces at himself in the mirror and walked out of the bathroom. He pulled on his exercise clothes, put on his sneakers, and left the apartment.

He did not know what time it was, and he had no interest in finding out. It was enough for him to know that it was morning, early morning. He leisurely jogged to the small park nearby and counted one thousand seven hundred thirty-four steps to the first water fountain. He planned to one day break his own record and run that distance at his top speed, without losing count of his steps.

He drank a little water and started jogging around the park. After one lap, he stopped and did his stretches. To catch his breath, he walked for a while. He decided to take a route back home that would pass by the bakery that made Barbari flatbreads. There were only four people standing on line. He greeted the baker who had glared at him the first few times he had gone there. He bought bread that was still hot from the kiln and sprinted all the way home. He ran into the landlady's brother in the doorway and said hello to him. The man stared at the bread and at his exercise clothes and said, "And you are?"

He did not want to ruin his good mood that morning. Trying to smile, he said, "I'm the new tenant. We met yesterday."

The man glowered at him and barked, "Do you think I'm crazy? Nuts? Aren't you the guy with the broken watermelon? Aren't you the klutz?" And as he walked out the door he shouted, "One of these days I'll hang myself and it'll be thanks to all of you and that old hag. She conned you and now you are conning me. And I blame it all on these university girls. If they held a protest and demonstrated, Hashemzadeh wouldn't dare face off with my sister and say whatever the hell he wants to the witch. Me, file a complaint? Me, take her to court?" He looked back and grumbled, "You're just like the rest of them. Don't you dare rip me off." Then he headed toward the park with the help of his cane and waved to him with his free hand.

Kamran hurried into the building and quickly crossed the ground-floor hallway. The voice of a woman on the radio or television wishing everyone a good morning had mixed in with the sound of fast western music coming from the university girls' apartment on the second floor. He could not understand why he had lost the energy and liveliness he had felt earlier.

He put the bread on the kitchen table and laid out his breakfast. Then he went back to the living room and began to exercise, vigorously and without pause, until he started to sweat again. By the time he had taken a shower and returned to the kitchen to eat, he was again feeling cheerful and lively. Mimicking the exaggerated motions of an opera singer, he took the kettle, filled it with water, and placed it on the stove, all the while whistling in harmony with his movements. While waiting for the water to boil, he drank a glass of cold milk and went to take a look at the ants' banquet. All that was left of the cockroaches was their hard shield-like shells, but the ants were still grappling with the chocolate and the pieces of sugar.

"Why didn't you finish these? Do you prefer cockroaches?" He went back to the kitchen to look for a cockroach. He did not find one. He opened the cabinet under the sink and looked inside and around the plastic bag he used as a trashcan. "You're out of luck," he said. "When I come back at noon, I'll try to find some other tasty food for you."

After breakfast, he smoked two cigarettes, sat on the easy chair, and thought about what to do that day. He did not have a swimming lesson, his time was all his, completely free. He could spend the day any way he liked. He thought it would not be a bad idea to make a round of the bookstores. He wrote in his agenda: *buy books*. That way, by the time he came back, half the day would have passed and it would be time for him to eat lunch. He remembered that there was a little macaroni left over from two nights ago. He went and took the pot out of the refrigerator, emptied it into the trash bag, and poured water in it for it to soak. He was relieved that he would most definitely have to spend some time preparing lunch. He scratched his head and thought for a while. There was a lot of food. He had red meat, chicken, mushrooms, fresh herbs, yogurt, tomatoes, cucumbers, and lettuce.

He decided to have yogurt with cucumbers for lunch so that he would not have to return home early to cook something. He went over to the sheet of paper and wrote: *Lunch, yogurt with cucumbers and mint*. He paused and then added: *with a little onion and black pepper.* If it were not for his messed-up stomach, he would have written "with plenty of onion and lots of black pepper"—both of which he loved. For his after-lunch activity, he wrote: *watch the houses and cars from the window, read, go to the park for a stroll, and, if possible, play soccer with the kids.*

If he did not take an afternoon nap, which he had resolved not to, he would be exhausted by the time he came back from the park, cooked dinner, and played with the ants of the Milky Way. He could therefore sleep soundly and wake up early enough the next morning to not miss the sunrise. Given all this, he would not give up his mornings and their routines for anything else in the world.

TWO

It was not unusual for the front door of the building to be open at that time of the night, an hour past sunset, but it was not usual either. He braced himself to rush through the ground-floor hallway so that he would not have to smell the putrid stench of trash that emanated from the apartment of the landlady's brother. He held his breath and quietly hurried to the staircase, and he breathed again only when he reached the first-floor landing. That way, he not only avoided suffering that horrid stink, but he also practiced increasing his lung capacity, which the swimming instructor had recommended. He stopped and let air into his lungs. He smelled meat patties, their scent mingled with the fragrance of a familiar perfume, but he could not remember where he had smelled it before and on whom. When he reached the second-floor landing, he saw a girl sitting on the stairs. As he walked past her, the whiff of her perfume reminded him of the broken watermelon and the game he had played a few days earlier. Just as before, she was dressed in brown from head to toe, and her loosely tied headscarf was barely covering her hair.

As soon as he walked into his apartment, he put the small lizard, which a few children had helped him catch in the park, next to the dead cockroaches on the ants' tray. "With all this fresh meat, you should have a party tonight."

For his own dinner, he thought it would not be a bad idea to prepare some kebab with the lamb's meat he had bought the day before. He also had fresh herbs, yogurt, and tomatoes. He did not feel like going all the way to the bathroom, so he just used some dish soap to wash his hands in the kitchen sink. He put the meat on the counter and cut it into chunks, enough for three full skewers. He grated an onion into a bowl and, while trying to wipe away his tears with his sleeve, mixed in some lemon juice and added the meat to the marinade. He looked at the bowl and in a silly, comical way appreciated his own housewifely skills. The meat would be tender by the time he took a shower and diddled away some time. Still, he wished he had put it to marinate at noon.

He stayed under the shower for a long time and played with the water drops. He slowly turned the knob until the water became very cold. He held his head under it and let it cascade over his ears. It was just like the times when he would submerge his head in the swimming pool and, except for a monotonous, continuous whirr, all other sounds would suddenly stop. It was then that he often wished he could inhale all the air in the world, so that he could stay underwater, naked and calm, listening to that soothing hum… not forever—he knew he bored easily—but long enough that he did not tire of it.

He stepped out of the shower feeling content and gratified. He was contemplating peace under water and massaging his scalp when he thought he heard a knock at the door. Thinking that the sound was probably coming from the downstairs apartment, he continued to rub his scalp. The likelihood of someone coming to see him was equal to that of a volcano erupting in the North Pole. The old landlady and her arrogant daughter always telephoned when they needed to speak with him, and he did not know anyone else.

Again, he heard the sound of knuckles rapping on a wooden door. He combed his hair back with his fingers and opened the door.

"Hello, sir."

It was the girl he had seen sitting on the stairs, with the same strong smell of perfume.

"I'm one of the tenants in the apartment downstairs. I've locked myself out, and my friends haven't come home yet. If it's no bother, may I wait for them here? Sitting on the stairs, well... you know what I mean. If the neighbors tell the landlady, she'll give me a hard time."

Surely, the girl's appearance at his door was not stranger than a volcano erupting in the North Pole, but why had she not gone to the tenant on the first floor? She seemed to be afraid of something. He let her in, closed the door, and motioned toward the sofa. "Please, have a seat."

She did not seem to notice the ants' feast. She walked past the tray, sat on one of the easy chairs, put down her handbag, and tried to straighten her coverall. Her headscarf slipped off, but she did not seem to care if a stranger saw her hair uncovered. He had occasionally seen the university girls. They were very careful about their hijab and wore full Islamic headdresses instead of headscarves. They seemed to be very observant, at least when they went outside.

"I can turn on the air conditioner if it is too warm for you here."

"I'd be grateful."

He turned on the air conditioner and set it on low. Then he went to the kitchen and used a plate to cover the bowl of marinating meat. "Would you prefer orange juice or melon juice?" he called out to the girl.

"I've troubled you enough. Just a glass of water would be fine."

He took two glasses, put an ice cube in each, and filled one with water and the other with orange juice. He set them on a plate—his tray was serving the ants—took it to the living room, and sat across from the girl.

"I have really imposed on you. I'm so sorry."

He stared at her and said, "No trouble at all. But how come your friends haven't come home yet?"

The girl picked up the glass of water and took a sip. "I don't know. They should have been back by now."

He would have to remember to wash off the smear of her heavy lipstick from the rim of the glass.

"Weren't you with them?" he asked.

She started playing with the square buttons on her brown coverall.

"I'm studying biology, they're studying chemistry. Our class schedules are different. I haven't seen them since after lunch."

The girl was nervously tugging at the buttons and twisting them. He wanted to ask her how she had managed to walk into the university without a full Islamic headdress and proper hijab. He did not ask her. It was none of his business and he did not care that she was lying. She had probably skipped her classes to go see her boyfriend.

"Don't worry," he said. "They'll show up soon."

"May I make a phone call?"

He took the telephone and put it next to her on the easy chair.

He went to the bedroom and without turning on the light stood at the window and looked out. The curtains of all nine apartments in the building across the street were closed, expect for the middle window on the second floor. All he could see inside were the vague outlines of a few frames on the wall. He thought about the small boy he had seen playing with his ball on the balcony the day before. The ball was still there, sitting in the corner.

He opened the window and leaned out to see if there was any light in the windows of the apartment downstairs. They were all dark. He went back to the living room. The girl's coverall and headscarf were lying on the floor next to her handbag. The light was on in the bathroom. He went and found a kitchen towel and covered the ants' banquet with it. He wondered why it was important for him that the girl not see it. She was just a girl, like all other girls. Was he trying to save his reputation from being ruined? Or what? It was ridiculous for him to want to appear as someone other than who he really was in front of a girl he did not know and might never see again. He took the kitchen towel and tossed it to the side.

He was starving. He went to the kitchen and took the rest of the meat out of the refrigerator and started cutting it into cubes. He cut enough for three more skewers of kebab.

"Would you like some help?"

The girl was standing next to the stone kitchen counter. She was wearing a pair of tight, dark blue pants and a short, open-necked shirt that barely came down to her waist.

He wondered if he would pay as much attention to women's figures if so many of them did not wear modest, loose coveralls out on the street.

"So, are you as hungry as I am?"

"A little," the girl said as she moved closer to him. "Now that I've imposed on you, what can I do to help?"

She was looking straight into his eyes. There was no sign of the shy nervousness he had sensed in her a few minutes earlier.

"The skewers are down there, second drawer to the right."

She had pulled back her dark hair into a simple ponytail. When she bent down, her shirt crept up and revealed her back.

"How many shall I bring?"

"Six."

The girl held the skewers under running water in the sink and said, "If it's for me, one is enough. I don't eat that much red meat."

He put the remainder of the lamb in the refrigerator. "Maybe I want to have five skewers," he said laughing. "Are you on a diet?"

"No, but I don't really like red meat all that much." She was carefully washing the skewers with sponge and dish soap, just like Fariba.

He was irritated that Fariba had suddenly entered his thoughts. He took the skewers from the girl and said, "They're clean. You don't have to wash them so obsessively."

He started skewering the marinated kebab.

"Did I do something wrong?" the girl asked.

He was angry with himself, and with the girl who had suddenly descended on him like doomsday. He could kick her out without caring whether her friends showed up or not. After all, it was not his fault that she had locked herself out of her apartment.

"I'm being a bother," the girl said. "I think I should leave." And she quickly gathered her things and left.

He heard her footsteps on the stairs. He tossed the skewers and the meat on the counter, closed his eyes, and took a deep breath. Clearly, it was not the girl's fault that he was intent on burying his past and never allowing it to reveal itself. The girl had just forgotten her keys. That was all. He was exasperated by his own outwardly sick and hysterical behavior. He could have acted calmly, allowed the girl to eat some dinner and then go on her way. And it was none of his concern whether she was lying or not. It was not his problem.

He pulled himself together, picked up a skewer, and started patiently piercing the meat, trying to forget what had just happened. He should not be so weak as to allow an incident as simple and as trivial as that to throw him off balance. He set the skewered meat aside and wiped his hands on his shirt. He got his Walkman and tried to find some upbeat music that was just that, upbeat. He did not find any. It had not occurred to him that someday he might need fast music. He put on his headphones and played *Kitaro's World of Music*. He went to the bedroom and lay down on the bed. That was why he liked Kitaro's music, long protracted melodies that were at times indistinguishable and progressed slowly and monotonously, so slowly that you would not realize the moment when they reached a crescendo, and suddenly it was the diminuendo, surprising and unexpected. Similar to life. Life itself.

He tried to coordinate the movements of his arms and legs, thrusting his arms forward in tandem with his kicks. When he touched the swimming pool floor, he relaxed his body so that he would float back up. Before reaching the surface, he realized he could hold his breath longer. He turned and again swam down to the bottom. He loved doing this. When he had first learned how to float in water, he had repeatedly dived to the bottom of the deepest section of the swimming pool without feeling the slightest bit tired. Now he wanted to swim to the bottom and return to the top twice in a row while holding his breath. He managed to touch the tiles on the pool floor for the second time, but, hard as he tried, he could not remove his hand from them. It was as if it had been nailed down. It was just like the time when, after practicing floating, the instructor had told him to empty his lungs and dive under water. In a depth of no more than one meter, his hand had gotten stuck to the bottom and no matter what he did he could not free it. Now, he grabbed his wrist with his other hand and pulled. He was running out of air. He tried harder. With his lungs depleted, his body started to shake. Something was clutching his throat and lungs and squeezing them. He was shaking his head violently, desperately trying to keep his mouth closed tight. With all his might he yanked his hand. He wanted to holler.

He was sitting up in bed, gasping loudly and rapidly. He did not know whether it was his own shout that had woken him up or the repeated knocks on the door. He wiped the sweat off his face, ran his fingers through his hair, and opened the door. The girl had come back.

"May I come in?"

He did not hesitate for a second. He stepped aside and let her in. The scent of her perfume had blended with the sharp smell of sweat. The back of her coverall was dusty. He put his Walkman and headphones on a stool, went to the bathroom and splashed water on his face and neck. He walked out without looking in the mirror. The girl was still standing by the door.

"Didn't you want to come in?"

"I lied to you." She was neither looking down, nor fiddling with her buttons. Her arms were hanging by her sides.

"Well?"

"It was all a lie. I'm not one of them." She pointed at the floor. "I was a guest in their apartment and they got fed up with me. They didn't come home tonight so that they can get rid of me. Or perhaps they're home and just won't open the door. Now what? May I come in?"

"You really got to me before. You put on a good show."

He went to the kitchen. The girl followed him.

"You're a nice guy. That's why I came back."

He laughed and turned to look at her. "How old are you?"

The girl came up to only slightly above his shoulder. "Twenty-three."

Her breath smelled bad. It smelled of an empty stomach. He took the bowl of extra meat and said, "You're still too young to know people after just one encounter. You've judged too quickly."

"You can't be a bad person."

"Thanks! Now come and give me a hand."

"Don't you want to know why I came back?"

Fed up, he swung around and snapped, "Would you like me to throw you out again?"

"You didn't throw me out. I went on my own."

"I really don't care why you left, why you came back, what you want, or even who you are. I'm just hungry. Do you understand?" He held up a skewer of meat and added, "I want to grill this and eat it. If you are hungry, too, come and help me so that we can eat sooner. Right now, this is the most important thing in the entire Milky Way."

One by one, he skewered more chunks of meat while secretly eyeing the girl. She walked out of the kitchen, took off her coverall and headscarf, and went and hung them on the coatrack. She glanced at the dust stain on the back of her coverall but ignored it. As she walked back, she pulled the rubber band out of her hair and snapped it around her wrist. She stood next to him and picked up a skewer. "Can I tell you something, if you won't get upset and throw me out?"

He did not want to talk. He continued to work in silence and did not look at her.

"You know, you put on an act just like me. Perhaps even more so."

"Do you always get so familiar this quickly?"

He salted the skewered meat and turned on the stove. He took two flatbreads out of the oven where he stored them and held them over the flame.

"You don't want to talk to me because you think I'm just a kid?"

He put the flatbreads on a plate and held two skewers over the flame.

"There are only two options if we are going to have a conversation." He took the other skewers from the girl. "We have to talk, not rattle nonsense. And, either I have to become as short as you, or you have to become as tall as me. Given that it is impossible for you to become any taller, I'm the one who has to do it, and I'm really not in the mood to bring myself down to your level. Can you fetch six tomatoes from the fridge?"

The smell and sizzling of the kebab made him even more faint with hunger. The girl brought three tomatoes and said, "Shall I wash them first or put them on a skewer as is?"

He ignored her sarcasm.

"Aren't you going to have any?"

"I don't like grilled tomatoes."

"Too bad. They're delicious."

The girl rinsed the tomatoes and skewered them. She went to turn on another flame on the stove.

"No, I'll do it myself. You wash some herbs and put two bowls of yogurt on the table."

He put the half-grilled skewered kebab between the two flatbreads on the plate, pressed down on them, and again held them over the flame. The girl had bent down and was looking around in the refrigerator. "Where are the herbs?"

"The bottom shelf, wrapped in a white cloth."

The girl put some of the herbs in a bowl and wrapped the rest back in the white cloth.

"Check and see if the cloth is still damp. If not, wet it a little."

"For someone who is so fussy about cleanliness, why did you get all steamed up when I was washing the skewers?"

"I'm not fussy. First of all, I don't want to have to go and buy a bunch of herbs every day. This way, they stay fresh and I can keep them for several days. Second, do me a favor and forget the whole issue with the skewers, and stop making snide remarks. Third, take the herbs out of the bowl, fill it with water, add two drops of dish soap, put the herbs back in, let them sit for a few minutes, then rinse and drain them."

The girl laughed. "You're perfect! Your wife is a lucky woman."

He did not laugh, and the girl grew quiet. The silence dragged on, the tomatoes grilled, the herbs and yogurt were set on the table, and they started to eat against the backdrop of a hush that was growing deeper and more protracted. The girl took a small taste of the tomatoes; a few drops of juice dripped on the table. He ignored it. The girl ignored it, too, or did not notice it. Perhaps it was the frown on his face that had made her not only stop chattering, but stop talking all together. They did not even exchange a glance. The ridiculous air that had settled on their even more ridiculous relationship was causing him inexplicable pain.

He did not speak until they had finished clearing the table. When the girl went to wash the dishes, he said, "Leave them. I'll wash them in the morning."

The girl did not react. She only said, "Don't you have a watch?"

"No."

He went to the bathroom to brush his teeth. He felt nauseated. Again, he did not look in the mirror. He did not brush his teeth either. He gargled with some water and walked out. The girl was sprawled on the sofa.

"That's going to be my place," he said. "Get up and go sleep in the bed."

He went and took the top sheet from the bed. The girl was standing behind him.

"I don't need a pillow," she said.

"Really?" He turned and looked at her. "Or did you say that because you just realized I only have one pillow?"

"I don't need to be very smart to see that you don't have anything other than a Walkman and a few tapes and an army of ants that you even hunt for. Do you always go to bed this early?"

He took the pillow. "The air conditioner is set on low. If it gets too warm for you, the control is over there." He pointed to the middle of the hallway.

"I won't be too warm. I usually sleep in the nude." And with her back turned to him, she took off her shirt. She was not wearing a bra. The skin between her shoulder blades was as white as marble. Clear and smooth.

"Good night."

He tossed the pillow on the sofa and said, "Will it bother you if I play some music?"

"Not if you turn the volume high enough for me to hear it, too."

He took out the *World of Music* tape and played meditation music. He turned off the lights, stretched out on the sofa, and put the sheet next to him for early morning.

"There's something I want to tell you. If I don't, it will keep eating away at me." The girl was standing in the bedroom door. She was covering her breasts with her shirt.

"That beard and mustache do not suit you at all."

Smiling, she turned off the bedroom light. The outline of her figure in the faint moonlight as she took off her pants and lay down on the bed with her back to the door, prominent and distinct, became subconsciously etched in his mind. He tried to surrender to the gentle melody of the music and to not think about the body he had seen. He knew that again he would not wake up in time to watch the sun rise. Consequently, he did not try to focus his thoughts on the hour he should wake and decided instead to give his internal clock a rest. He promised himself he would not miss the sunrise the following morning. He thought about the dawning sun and the peaceful moments that awaited him.

The sound of the telephone ringing jolted him awake. By the time he got up and answered it, while sluggishly massaging his back, which ached because of the night he had spent on the sofa, the jangle of the tiny mallet in the receiver had blared in his head three more times.

"Hello?..." There was no answer. Again, he said, "Hello?..."

It was light outside. He rubbed his eyes and yawned. He had to remember to unplug the telephone at night and to replace that ancient unit. The old landlady had left it for him, expecting deep gratitude in return.

That early in the morning, it did not occur to him that someone might have misdialed a number. He rubbed his back more vigorously. He stretched his neck and grunted. The telephone rang again. Ignoring his pain, he leaped up and unplugged it. But then he thought it might not be a bad idea to give the caller a hard time. He reconnected the telephone and answered it.

"Hello?…"

"Now I know for sure you're awake, Mr. Lazy. Didn't you want to watch the sun rise? If you don't move fast, you'll miss it again. And thanks for your hospitality last night, my darling. Of course, you won't be my darling until you get rid of that comical beard. Bye!"

He was stunned. He had not even had a chance to say hello a second time. He tapped on the switch hook a few times. He hung up and rushed over to the bedroom. The sheet, neatly folded, was at the foot of the bed and there was no sign of the girl.

He thought hard, but he could not remember having said anything to her about wanting to see the sunrise.

THREE

He hollered and roared as much as he could. There was no sound that he did not make, yelling at the top of his lungs. His vocal cords felt like they were about to tear. It made little difference whether Esteghlal was on the offensive or Persepolis; just the fact that the crowd rose to its feet and shouted at will, cursed at the referee, and hurled all sorts of usual and unusual things at the players was enough for him to lose himself among them, to howl as loudly as he could, and to revel in the fact that he was not even a tiny fraction of that multitude.

Other than satisfying a sense of nostalgia, the only reason he was at the stadium, watching the boring and idiotic match between two of the country's most popular soccer teams, was so that he could transform into an insignificant speck among a raucous crowd of more than a hundred thousand and shout on and on without anyone complaining.

When he left the stadium, he cared neither about his hoarse voice and sore throat, nor about his stomach that was stuffed with sunflower seeds, ice cream, and soda—all of which he had stopped eating years ago. Like a carefree man walking on clouds, he decided to stroll as far as Azadi Circle without questioning what he was hoping to find at that hour of the night, walking alongside the highway and against the direction of cars traveling at breakneck speed.

He did not know how long he had walked. By the time he came to himself, there was nothing in the dark in the middle of nowhere but the bright headlights of oncoming cars and the drawn out blare of their horns. He added his success in crossing the highway in one piece to the list of small blessings in his life. Now he could complete that pitiful image by waving at the headlights hissing by. When a pair of them pulled over about a hundred and fifty meters away, he ran toward them like an excited child.

"Azadi?"

"Hop in, man."

There were no other passengers in the car.

"What are you doing around these parts at this hour of the night? Buddy, your fate is cockeyed, just like mine... or were you out there looking for a grain of decency?"

The man laughed out loud and turned up the volume on the radio. The singer kept repeating, "Farewell... farewell..."

"What's her name?"

The man slapped the steering wheel. "Heh! When I say my fate is cockeyed, don't tell me it isn't. Look who I get stuck with in this damned life. Buddy, she's one of those crooners in Los Angeles, which they're calling "Tehrangeles" these days, owing to all the Iranians living there. What do you do for a living?"

"Loaf around."

"My kind of guy. The minute I saw you, I said to myself, 'Give him a ride, listen to someone talk a few big words, the guy looks like he's a somebody.' But it looks like I hit the hay trough. On my life, don't you go taking it bad. I'm just pulling your leg to cheer you up. Screw everything, tune it all out..."

"No, you're absolutely right."

"Now you're piling it on... are you into letting loose and living it up?"

"Do I look like I am?"

"If you are, I've got whatever you want. Ope, tar, dope..."

"Thanks."

"Thanks what? Yes or no? I'll give it away at a bargain."

"I have no money. Will you treat?"

Again, the man slapped the steering wheel. "Huh, and I thought you're not that kind of guy. My good man, my decent chum, what can I say? In these crooked times, even a wife doesn't give it to her husband free."

The man rattled nonsense all the way to Azadi Circle. Then he charged him double the normal fare and drove off.

He so wanted to sleep.

He checked on the ants, caught a cockroach for them, and had no appetite for dinner. He stood at the window and ignored his toothache. He looked out at the darkness of the night hovering above. There was no one on the second-floor balcony of the brick building. None of the windows of that apartment were lit. He had only seen the young boy once, and he could not understand why, every time he looked at that building, he remembered the ball being tossed out onto the balcony. It was still there. All the lights were on in the apartment below; in one of the windows, which he assumed was the living room, colorful lights were flickering on and off behind lace curtains. A man walked out onto the balcony. Laughing, he picked up something that looked like a brazier and carried it inside. Through the door that remained ajar, he saw a few boys and girls dancing. He could hear jazz music. The man came back and closed the door. The sound of the music faded away. He was thinking that, right about then, one of the neighbors was going to call the police so that the fanatic patrol guards would raid the party and make a mess of it.

He turned out all the lights, got his Walkman, and lay down on his bed. He listened to Clayderman's music to block out the noise the university girls were making downstairs—it traveled through the air conditioning duct. He felt like rolling onto his left side. He took off the headphones, turned the volume to maximum, and closed his eyes, wanting to think about nothing other than the sound of the piano and percussion. There was the distant chant of a chorus of women singing in the background. He tried to isolate it so that he could focus on the women, innocently standing somewhere on stage, their gaze shifting from their sheet music to the conductor's hands. Perhaps one of them was suffering from a faint toothache that was not painful enough to stop her from keeping in tune with the others.

If only he could sleep. The tape reached a piece of music that he did not like at all, a silly melody with a fast tempo, occasionally accompanied by soft chimes that sounded like bells on a goat standing on its hind legs, its forelegs on a tree, trying to tear off a few branches and leaves. He turned off the Walkman. At that moment, whatever music he listened to, he was likely to discover a sound resembling goat bells or the braying of a donkey even in its foreground.

He went to the kitchen and held his mouth under the sink faucet and drank so much water that he ran out of breath. He turned off the water and, with a rapid puff, sucked air into his lungs, then wiped his mouth with the back of his hand. He got dressed, went out, and just walked, for no particular reason and with no particular destination.

At the end of the road, he saw a string of colorful lights. When he reached the three-way intersection, he turned onto the main street. He lit a cigarette and passed under an ornate, brightly lit triumphal arch. A banner tied to two of the sycamore trees flanking the street read, "Felicitations to all Shias of the world on the auspicious birthdate of Imam Zaman...," and before he could finish reading the sentence, he passed under the banner and continued walking. He passed a few stores that were closed and arrived at a sandwich shop that was open. He stopped. He had not eaten since noon, but he still had no appetite. There was a coffee shop across the street. He thought perhaps a glass of fruit juice would change the unpleasant taste in his mouth, allowing him to smoke another cigarette. He had to remember to buy chewing gum.

He sat at a table in the outdoor seating area and ordered a glass of melon juice and a pack of PK chewing gum. The young waiter who took his order hid his surprise behind a dutiful smile and walked away. How he hated plastic tables and chairs. He cautiously leaned back and watched the young couple gazing into each other's eyes at a table farther away. He heard a woman laughing behind him. He turned and looked. The woman had her back to him; there were two young men sitting with her. Waiting for the melon juice, he counted the nine tables and thirty chairs that were there. Three of the tables had only two chairs, like his table and the one the young couple were sitting at. But the table with three customers sitting at it was a table for four. Again, he heard the woman laugh. She said, "That's not enough for two."

The young waiter brought the melon juice. He had put the pack of chewing gum on a plate next to the glass. He took a sip of the juice and listened to the woman. "After you graduate, after you get a job, come see me with money in your pockets. Okay?"

"But where are you going?" one of the young men complained. "We can come to some sort of an agreement."

The other one said, "Let her go. Let her get lost... the cunt."

He looked at the woman's profile as she walked onto the sidewalk and passed the colorful blinking lights. He took another sip, got up, paid for the juice and chewing gum, and, without looking at the young men who were still cursing the woman, quickly began to follow her.

He walked faster and, a few steps away from the woman, took out his pack of cigarettes. He adjusted his speed to walk next to her, in step with her. He lit his cigarette and looked at her. She had turned and was staring at him.

"Will you come with me?"

He could not say she was pretty, but she was not ugly either. Same height as him, a round face and chubby cheeks. Her bright red lipstick made her lips stand out. He did not regret his accidental choice, especially since he liked women who were as tall as he was.

"Your place or mine?"

"Mine."

"You alone?"

He blew out the cigarette smoke. "Yep."

"Thirty thousand, all night."

She protracted "all night" enough to make it worth thirty thousand tomans.

"That's too steep, but fine. I've never haggled over anything in my life."

"I could bite you!" the woman said laughing. "Where've you been all my life?"

He wanted to laugh, too. "I mean, I don't know how."

"I'll teach you tonight." She nodded toward the street. "Won't you get a taxi for us?"

"Are you in a hurry?"

"What would a drifter like me be in a hurry for? I mean because of the police patrols."

"My apartment is close by."

"Tonight they're putting the squeeze on. Just in the past hour, they've driven by several times."

"Given my age and this bushy beard, no one is going to suspect me. They're after the kids."

"You don't know these bastards. They don't give a damn about these things. They get a kick out of hounding people. They're all a bunch of lunatics with hang-ups."

"Who doesn't have hang-ups?" He tossed away his cigarette butt. "I'll walk ahead and leave the front door open. Third floor."

"Single unit per floor?"

"Yes."

He picked up his pace and lit another cigarette. His mouth still tasted nasty, just as he still had no appetite, just as all the other "stills" piled up in his life.

He drank a glass of cold water and went back to the bedroom. There was still some time before sunrise. The sheet had slipped off of the woman's body as she slept, curled up and facing the wall. She was not fat, but filled out to the point that her thighs and behind looked like a flat desert road, even and without bumps. The previous night, as he was caressing her, he had asked, "But where's your butt?"

"They ate it until it was finished. But you can eat these instead." And cackling, she had shoved a pair of huge, sagging sacks in his face.

He could have pulled the sheet back over her, as he used to do when he would wake up and see that the blanket had fallen away from Fariba. He went back to the kitchen. The itch in his throat, the result of all the shouting at the stadium, was bothering him. He poured some water in the kettle, set it on the stove, and waited for it to come to a boil. He sat at the kitchen table and gazed at the patterns on its surface. There was a dried-up blotch on it. He ran his finger over it and remembered two nights ago, when he had eaten kebab with the girl and she had picked at a tomato. He wet a rag and scrubbed the spot. There was still a faint stain. With the other side of the rag, he wiped the entire table and was happy that the stain disappeared.

He took the boiling kettle off the stove. He put a spoonful of honey in a glass, washed two large lemons, cut them in half, and squeezed their juice over the honey. Then he filled the glass with hot water and stirred it well. He sat at the table and drank the concoction one sip at a time. He swallowed and took a deep breath. His throat felt less gravelly. He took his pack of cigarettes, drank another sip of the mixture, and smoked two cigarettes one after the other. After he finished his drink, he remained sitting there for a long time. He tried to block out the woman's monotonous breathing that in the dead silence of the morning had replaced the kettle's gurgling.

He got up and went to the closet, unzipped his duffel bag, and took thirty one thousand–toman bills from his wallet. He was about to close the bag when, again, like every time he opened it, he put his hand inside and felt the bottom to make sure that his thirty-five thousand dollars was still there. He closed the zipper, went to the bedroom, pulled the sheet off the woman's legs, and said, "Hey, wake up."

The woman half-opened her eyes and muttered, "What is it?"

"Get up. It's time to go. It's morning."

The woman grimaced and sniffed. "I'm sleepy."

"Enough sleep. Come on, get up."

He yanked her arm. Dazed and confused, the woman sat up. "What happened?"

He tossed the money at her and gathered her clothes.

"Get dressed and get out of here."

He went back to the kitchen, poured himself a glass of milk, and drank it slowly. The woman got dressed and, still looking drowsy, came and stood in the kitchen door. "What the heck happened to you all of a sudden?"

He gulped down the rest of the milk, and went and opened the front door. "Take care."

The woman did not move.

"Shall I come back tonight?"

"No."

She slung her handbag over her shoulder and put her shoes next to each other in front of her feet. "I'll charge you less."

"Thanks."

"Shall I come?"

"I said no."

She slipped on her right shoe.

"At least let me eat some breakfast before I go. Not even stray dogs leave their holes at this hour."

"I'm all out of breakfast."

The woman put on her other shoe and walked out. "The hell with you, you nutcase, with your disgusting cockroaches and ants."

He closed the door and lit another cigarette.

———————————

He was wearing his exercise clothes when he went up to the rooftop. He stood in the center of it and did not move until the sun came up. He felt faint as he was going back down to his apartment. He stopped for a moment and then continued making his way down the stairs. He did not want to cancel his morning exercise. He jogged to the park without a break and, on his way to the water fountain, twice miscounted his steps. He decided that if he did not feel up to running laps around the park and doing his stretches, he would just buy his daily Barbari bread from the bakery and absentmindedly eat half of it on the way home, and then he would go straight to the bathroom and take a shower.

His lingering under the shower was not as it always was either. He sensed it. He took a towel and, before stepping out, stopped and stared for a while at his ears, nose, eyes, cheeks, and hair. He ran his hand over his beard and noticed a few white strands under his chin.

Not eating breakfast, which he had no craving for, forced him to pick up his agenda. He stared at a blank page while chewing the end of his pencil, anxious over how to pass the hours until his swimming lesson, and how to bear his maddening frustration, which could have been brought on by the girl leaving or by the absurd monotony that like an octopus was slithering closer and casting a horrible shadow over the seemingly endless minutes and hours.

He was in the mood neither for his swimming lesson—how many sessions had he missed? —nor for reading, or… He wondered if there was anything at all he felt like doing. He even considered going to a music class, a silly notion that had now and then popped into his mind. What instrument should he choose? The piano or the guitar that had beautiful names, or the two- or three-stringed tar that could perhaps instill an air of sage-like mysticism in him. He had always come to the conclusion that he should opt for the triangle, because it seemed to be an easy instrument to play and equally as easy to learn. And, more important, because it was unlikely that he would find a school that offered triangle lessons, which gave him a reason to give up on the idea altogether.

He tossed his agenda to the side and went to see the tireless ants that were still laboring around the jam, the sugar, and the cockroach, without ever stopping to rest. He caught two more cockroaches for them and sat down to smoke another cigarette. Then he got dressed and went out. He passed an old woman cleaning the staircase. A few steps farther down, he noticed that she was following him and mopping his footprints off the wet stairs. She was doing this so intently that it seemed as if wiping away each footprint required a century of time and a world of energy. He went down two more steps and realized he was still leaving traces behind. He rubbed his foot in a few drops of water that had gathered in a corner. The water turned muddy. He turned around, smiled at the old woman, and said, "I was exercising in the park this morning. My shoes got dirty."

The old woman did not even glance at him.

He went back up the stairs, took the rag that was hanging over the rim of a bucket of water, walked backward down the stairs and wiped his shoeprints as he went.

"I'll clean it myself," the old woman said.

As he moved down another step, he replied, "I'll leave the rag on the bottom step." He paused. "How much do you get paid to mop this place?"

"Ten thousand a month."

"To clean every day?"

"One day yes, one day no."

"Do you know that to clean my footprints you have to climb down thirty-two steps? Have you ever counted them?"

The old woman bit her lip. "What? I'm not nosy. Instead of this nonsense, go buy a mat and put it outside your door. No need for you to feel sorry for me."

"Okay, I'll buy one," he said laughing. "But why are you getting angry?"

He put the rag on a step and, ignoring the old woman, walked down and looked at his footprints as they grew fainter. He walked down the street and tried not to think about anything. He did not know where he was going, and he did not want to know. He sat down on a ledge outside a shop, lit a cigarette, and watched the people. He could not tell whether they were going to or coming from someplace. He guessed that, relative to himself, the man wearing a suit on such a hot day and talking on his cell phone was at that moment coming. But if he waited for him to pass by, then he would probably be going. Of course, again, relative to himself. Given this, he could determine whether every person was coming from or going to someplace.

He decided he was contemplating a stupid issue, because even if he spent a hundred years watching all the people walking along the sidewalk, he still would not know where they were going. He could only guess—an amusing pastime for someone like him who sometimes became terribly muddled because of all the free time he had and did not know what to do with. He shot his cigarette butt into the street gutter like a marble and stared at the passersby to choose one of them. When he focused on the hordes of people and their appearances, he realized that selecting one of them would not be easy, especially since he had not come up with any standards or criteria. He decided to leave it all up to chance and to follow the first person that was not carrying a dark blue, black, or beige bag. Man or woman, of any age. He saw a man wearing glasses and carrying a dark brown briefcase with red piping on it. The hair on the crown of the man's head had grown a bit sparse. He was happy that the man was neither very young nor middle-aged, because it made it more difficult to guess where he was going, and the game would be more fun. He set off a few steps behind him. The man turned onto a road near the next intersection and then onto another road. He stopped in front of an apartment building with a black façade and pressed a doorbell. Kamran stood behind a tree and watched to make sure the door would open and the man would go inside. That was not fun. He decided to go back to the main street, but instead he continued along that same road and passed in front of the apartment building. As he was going around the corner at the end of the road, he stopped to see if there were any people nearby, other than the woman who was carrying a plastic bag and most likely on her way home. A little farther ahead, a man and a woman turned onto the road and, while arguing, got into a dilapidated Peugeot.

He turned onto a main street that was more crowded. This time, he picked a man who was about forty years old. The man did not have a briefcase and was not wearing eyeglasses. He was dressed in a plain, light-colored shirt and a pair of black trousers. A tad taller than him, borderline handsome, and walking at a brisk pace, which could make discovering his destination interesting. In step with the man, but a few meters back, he walked fast and felt somewhat excited by his pretended haste. Farther ahead, the man crossed the street and walked into a coffeehouse with a large neon sign: *Toranj*.

He followed the man inside, but did not instantly see him there. He saw a small sign on the wall made from a slice of tree trunk: *A Family Establishment*. He sat at a table, ordered a glass of carrot juice, and waited. Perhaps, unbeknownst to his wife, the man was there to meet his lover. Perhaps he was not married. Then why had he not invited his girlfriend to his home? He probably could not, or maybe it was the first time they were meeting and it was not proper for him to invite her to his place. Or perhaps the woman had not agreed to go there.

He had barely drunk half of his carrot juice when the man, wearing a white smock, emerged from behind a large refrigerator and started gathering the bowls of sauce from the tables. He slowly sipped the rest of his carrot juice and paid no attention to the man's conversation with another man who was standing behind the counter, tossing large carrots into a basin.

He positioned himself so that the man would not see him. He seemed to have grown suspicious. What had attracted Kamran's attention and driven him to shadow that man, apart from being about the same age as him and hence somehow his equal, was not the man's neatly trimmed beard and simple clothes. Nor was it his slight limp that made him drag his left foot, which he needlessly tried to conceal, as it was in fact not noticeable at first glance. And it was not the innocent sheepish expression in his eyes, which became noticeable only after one's attention was drawn to the medium-size mole in the corner of his eye. Each one of those factors could have driven him to automatically follow the man, but, more than anything else, what had compelled him was the strange, indescribable feeling the man triggered in him.

After trailing him for more than an hour, Kamran realized that the man was simply wandering around, just as he himself used to do. He was sure he had found someone who meekly walked with his head down, but did not leave his home to go to work, perhaps to buy or not to buy something on the way, or to occasionally go to or not go to the cinema. He was someone who, other than a few places, had nowhere to go—something he may not even be aware of—someone who never considered the fact that he could have a purpose or a goal, even if it were only an entertaining game that sooner or later he would abandon for the sake of another one. And for that reason, Kamran did not leave the man and continued to follow him at a shorter distance. It was at the bus stop that their eyes met for an instant and Kamran was forced to move away from him and stand behind the crowd, but in such a way that he could still see him.

Before they got off the bus, he looked at the man one more time. Just like the other standing passengers, he was holding onto the support bar above him, and just like them, he was slightly leaning over the person sitting in front of him. Out on the street, Kamran hesitated, he wanted to stop tailing someone who sometimes was and sometimes was not like everyone else. His pause put greater distance between them, but he continued following the man as he turned a corner, went to the bank, bought a few odds and ends from a shop, and entered a three-story apartment building on a quiet road. Kamran moved closer to the building so that he could watch it more carefully. Perhaps seeing a curtain move or a window open would help him figure out what floor the man lived on.

He wandered around there for an hour, until he became certain that the man was not likely to go out again, especially not at noon. He went to a sandwich shop he had passed earlier, ordered a plain bologna sandwich, and ate it as he walked back to the building. He swallowed the last bite as he positioned himself near the man's home. He looked up and down the road. There was no one else there. He kicked an empty soda can that, just like him, was there for no reason, or perhaps was there for a reason. Imagining an escape from all constraints, achieving a sort of freedom from the tedious path of simple and seemingly mundane events, and preferring that to the confining and senseless worries and anxieties of life, was starting to lose its appeal. Little by little, the pleasant numbness he had felt in the beginning was turning into the mind-numbing dreariness he had escaped from. He kicked the can again. He could kick it a few more times, until, clanking along on a meaningless and humid summer afternoon, it would fall into the mix of mud and algae in the street gutter. Who knew when water would flow through to wash it away, or not wash it away? He picked up the can and stood there for a long time. Standing on an empty road and contemplating a can was no more ridiculous than following people around for lack of anything else to do. In his state, he did not care whether musing over a can was meaningful or meaningless.

He remembered the ball on the balcony. Every time he had seen it in recent days, it had reminded him of the little boy and his mother's frizzy, disheveled hair.

FOUR

It could not have been past 7:00 a.m. He did not hear any sounds. He gently knocked on the door and waited.

"Who is it?"

It was the sleepy voice of a young woman.

"I'm your upstairs neighbor."

It took a while for the girl to open the door. She had tried to cover her tousled hair under a headscarf. A few chestnut strands were stuck to her forehead, above her puffy eyes.

"I'm terribly sorry to bother you at this hour of the morning, but I need to see your roommate. She told me her name but, unfortunately, I have forgotten it. The young lady who always wears a brown coverall."

"Oh, you mean Nahid."

"Is she home?"

"She's not our roommate, she's Atefeh's friend, she stayed with us for only a short time. She doesn't come here any more. Is there something I can help you with?"

"Yes. It's quite urgent. Could I ask you to pass on a message to her?"

The girl blinked a few times. "I don't know where she is. She hasn't been coming to the university for a while. But, wait…"

She left the door ajar. He could hear her call, "Atefeh… Atefeh…"

He saw a corner of the living room. Similar to his apartment, it had light-colored carpeting. He peeked in, but did not see anything else. He heard the same girl's muffled voice. "It's the guy who goes jogging every morning. I don't know what he wants with her."

The other girl, with frizzy blond hair and fair skin, had thrown a shawl over her bare shoulders and was not that intent on covering her cleavage.

"What do you want with Nahid, sir?"

Her sharp tone was accompanied by a sleepy yet piercing look. The first girl came and stood behind her.

"As I explained to your friend, I would not have bothered you if it were not an important matter."

"Nahid doesn't come here anymore." She looked at him even more sharply and spoke fast. "To be honest, I don't let her come, and I have no news of her."

"You don't see her at the university either?"

"She hasn't been there in two weeks. Is there anything else?"

She closed the door slightly.

"I told you, it is a very, very urgent issue." He decided to try his luck by adding a second "very."

"Do you have her address?"

"What do you want her address for?"

She pushed the door farther shut and spoke in an abrupt tone that was not far from a "no."

"Look here, young lady. I'm not an idle do-nothing to drop everything and go knocking on doors looking for her highness." He was stunned by his own sudden curtness. "I can find her with the help of detectives from the police department. Being her close friend, you're probably tangled up in all this, too. She stole fifteen million tomans in Travelers Checks from me and took off. Would you suggest I not look for her? If I don't find her, I will drag you to the police station instead. It's up to you."

The girl standing in the back was about to burst into tears. "Sir," she pleaded. "I swear on the Quran, we know nothing. We don't know her all that well. She spent a few nights here and then we kicked her out. If she were to show up again, we wouldn't let her in. And I swear we have no news of her."

The frizzy-haired girl gave him the name of a street and said, "I've gone to her place many times, but I don't know the house number. It's a large cream-colored door with blue frosted-glass panels and lights on either side."

"If by any chance she drops by to see you, you'll let me know. Right?"

The girl in the back, who was clearly frightened, said, "You can be sure, sir. Just please don't drag us into this. It's that floozy's doing." She glanced at her friend. "Maybe she's the one who stole Maryam's money, too. Nahid was here the night her money disappeared."

As he was about to leave, he heard voices coming from downstairs. Two people were talking loudly. The frizzy-haired girl, who was now trying to keep the shawl tightly draped over her bare chest, said, "I just remembered... there's a small park near her home."

One of the voices coming from downstairs turned into a scream. "You dragged me all the way here just to tell me this?"

The first girl said, "It's the landlady."

"They're having a fight again," the other one said.

He thought, the old landlady was so short that she barely came up to burly Hashemzadeh's chest, but her voice was ten times louder than his.

"Lady, what do you mean, 'just this,' we're suffering from the stench. How long are we supposed to put up with it?"

"Then how come the others don't complain?"

"That's their business. Maybe they all have a cold and are congested. I will file a complaint."

He heard a door being slammed shut.

He hated wide avenues, especially crowded ones.

He easily found the building. Five floors, with a white façade. He rang the third doorbell on the right: Manouchehri. He thought about the excuse he had to come up with for being there. He rang again and stepped back to look up at the windows on the third floor. The lace curtains on all the windows were drawn. From above his sunglasses, he saw the silvery tip of the window-guard. It was shining in the bright sunlight.

The third time he pressed the bell, he held it down and counted to ten. Then he rang the bell for the apartment next door. The faded label read: Ebrahimian. He wondered, if again no one answers, should he ring the bell of an apartment on the second floor or the fourth floor?

"Who is it?"

It was a woman's voice, mature, probably over fifty, fifty-five.

"I'm terribly sorry to disturb you. I need to see your neighbor, Mr. Manouchehri. I've been ringing his doorbell, but no one answers. Would you happen to know where he is?"

"And you are?"

"I'm one of his relatives. I'm visiting from the provinces."

"If you are a relative, then how come you don't know that Mr. Manouchehri passed away two years ago? Instead of harassing people, you should stay in touch with your family."

Before disconnecting, he heard the woman say, "What characters!..."

He walked away and, before reaching the small park, stopped at a convenience store and bought a cold soda, a slice of cake, and some chewing gum. He walked along the stone ledge bordering the park and picked a location that had a view of the building. It was no more than five hundred meters away. He sat under a bulky advertisement pillar and tried to squeeze his entire body under its ten-inch-wide shadow. It was close to noon. Or perhaps it was noon. He would wait.

He was surprised to see an old man and a small boy playing soccer under the hot sun. The boy was intent on dribbling and passing the ball between the old man's legs. The old man was keeping his feet together and struggling to not let the ball through. He leaned away from the hot pillar, twisted the cap on the soda bottle, and listened to it hiss. A boy and a girl were sitting together on the other side of the park, batting eyes at each other. The boy tried to take the girl's hand. The girl pulled away, but not in a way that would offend the boy. He thought about all the boys and girls he was seeing lately, just sitting and staring into each other's eyes. He ate his cake as slowly as he could. The soda bottle was still half-full.

An eight- or nine-year-old boy walked out of the apartment building and wanted to cross the street. The cars were driving by at high speed. Living on a one-way, six-lane street in the city center, with all that noise, was the stupidest decision, and one that you would only make under pressure.

The boy was not far from the intersection, perhaps seven or eight hundred meters. He was biding his time, waiting for the lights to change and the traffic to slow down. Then he calmly crossed the street. He appreciated the determined look on the boy's face and followed him with his eyes until he walked into the convenience store. He tossed the soda bottle and the cake wrapping into the trashcan and again looked over at the young man who had still not succeeded in taking the girl's hand. He went back to the convenience store and stood where he could continue to keep an eye on the apartment building. The boy was reading from a piece of paper he was holding.

"And two bags of macaroni."

The shopkeeper went over to one of the shelves.

"A box of tissues. And four pieces of Hobi chocolate. Mom said you should give me the big ones."

The shopkeeper put the macaroni and the box of tissues in a plastic bag and said, "Let me see your list."

The boy took a step back.

"What for?"

"There'll be no chocolates if you don't let me see it."

"Come on! Mom always puts chocolate on the list. This time she wrote four, I swear to God."

"Don't swear in vain, my boy. It's a sin."

"Okay, I won't. Give me four pieces of Hobi chocolates."

The shopkeeper brought four pieces of chocolate and put them on the counter. "Here's the chocolate. Now, give me the list."

"She wrote the big ones."

"Don't make me call her."

"If you love your kids, you'll stop hassling me. For once, listen to me. How much would three pieces cost?"

"I can't. Your mother will come and tell me off."

"I won't tell her."

"And the money?"

Still standing there, with his eyes on the front door of the apartment building, Kamran said, "Sir, could I please have four pieces of Hobi chocolate?" And he turned and winked at the boy.

The shopkeeper eyed him warily and weighed the chocolate on the balance scale. He put them in a bag and said, "Here you are, sir."

"Then just give me one piece," the boy persisted.

The shopkeeper gave him a piece of chocolate. The boy took it and the plastic bag. "I'm going now. But this isn't how friends are supposed to be."

The boy had left the store by the time Kamran paid for the chocolates. "Kids these days are such brats."

The boy was standing at the curb, waiting for the traffic to slow down. Kamran tried to give him the chocolates, but he would not take them.

"First tell me what they're for."

"For friendship. So that you and I can be friends."

"You think you're dealing with a kid? I'm ten. I'll leave if you don't tell me what you really want. And I'm not a beggar. We can make a trade."

"Man-to-man promise?"

The boy nodded toward the convenience store and said, "I'm not like some people."

"A real promise? And, you can't tell anyone about it."

The boy opened his eyes wide and said, "It's a secret?" He winked and added, "Just like in the movies. Now, don't drag it out. Tell me what you want, and I'll see if it's worth four chocolates. It may cost you more. I won't let you cheat me."

"What I need is worth one piece of chocolate," Kamran said laughing.

"Then why did you buy four?"

"I like chocolates, too. Is your last name Ebrahimian?"

"No, they live upstairs from us."

"I thought so. You couldn't possibly be that foul-tempered guy's son."

The boy's attention was on the chocolates.

"Hand them over." He held out his hand.

"That wasn't what I wanted."

"One chocolate per question. Deal?"

"Only if every answer is worth one chocolate. You'll have to tell me everything you know. And the question I already asked doesn't count. It wouldn't be fair, because I didn't know you expected one chocolate per question when I asked it. Like gentlemen, we first have to set the terms and then start."

"Okay. I agree. Like gentlemen. You told me your terms. My term is that I first get the chocolate, then I'll answer the question."

"Fine. Let's shake on it."

They shook hands. He looked over at the apartment building, gave the boy a piece of chocolate, and asked, "Tell me about the Manouchehri family."

"About all of them? Or just Nahid?"

"You rascal! Do you want a chocolate or not? Tell me about Nahid."

"Give me the other three, too, and I'll tell you everything you want to know about her. Man to man."

He handed him the three chocolates. "Well?"

"First of all, she's walking this way. Look."

He pointed to the other side of the street. She was dressed in blue from head to toe. He suddenly felt rattled and did not know what to do. Trying to regain his composure, he turned and walked toward the convenience store, doing his best to keep his back to the street. The boy called out, "But I haven't told you anything yet!"

As he was walking away, he said, "No need. The chocolates are yours."

He walked into the store. The shopkeeper gave him a sideways look.

"One chocolate milk."

Her clothes were three different shades of blue. Her pants and headscarf were darker than her coverall. She was chatting with the boy. Then the boy pointed to the store. He pulled himself to the side. The girl laughed and the two of them went inside the apartment building.

He gulped down the chocolate milk. The shopkeeper said, "If this heat has made you thirsty, that's not going to help."

He paid, walked out, and lit a cigarette. The old man and the boy he had seen in the park were walking toward the intersection. The boy was probably the old man's grandson. He watched them as they waited for the light to turn red and followed them with his eyes as they walked across the crosswalk and onto a street on the other side. If he were in the right mood, he would have followed them, and along the way tried to guess what floor of their building they lived on.

Waiting there was useless. He decided to go back, ring the doorbell, and talk to the girl. What would he say? He thought of inviting her for a cup of tea or coffee. He waited for the traffic to slow down. The boy and girl in the park were still sitting there. He saw two Basiji guards on motorcycles pull up in front of them. Both had sparse beards and were wearing army uniforms. They were barely twenty. Shaken and nervous, the boy and girl leaped up. He could guess the initial questions and answers: Are you two related? Do your parents know you are together? And then they would probably harass the girl because she was wearing lipstick and a close-fitting coverall, and the guy because of his hair style and his short-sleeved T-shirt with an English word on it—to the Basijis, it was graphic proof of the invasion of Western culture.

The guards separated the boy and girl, took each one to a different side, and started interrogating them. They wanted to see if they would give matching answers to similar questions. That was stage one. If they passed, then the Basijis would call the girl's parents and question them over the telephone. Now the parents would have to come up with answers that corresponded with what the girl and boy had said. The slightest divergence would result in the young couple's arrest and prosecution. He knew a few couples that the court had actually forced into marriage. There were, however, lenient judges who demanded only a commitment to marry, and beyond that, they did not care. Sometimes, the Basiji guards would pick up the girls, have their fun with them, and then let them go. Over the years, Kamran had seen and heard it all.

He was crossing the street and watching the interrogation when he heard the sharp screech of a car braking. For an instant, he felt he was in the air and everything was whirling around him. And then he felt nothing at all.

FIVE

At first, he saw nothing. He only heard what sounded like a drone underwater. He had a sense of absolute freedom, but did not know where it emanated from. He felt he was floating in a soft, fluffy mass. He was drifting in it and wanted to glide even faster when suddenly he crashed into a cement wall. It was like diving into a one-centimeter-deep swimming pool.

A bright light forced the muscles in his eyes to contract. A cluster of white slowly became visible. A finger released his eyelid so that his eye could close. He felt a thousand-kilo weight on his chest. He opened his eyes and blinked a few times. He remembered the street and the scorching sun at noon. He remembered the Hobi chocolates. He recognized the smell of the hospital and realized that the thousand-kilo weight on his chest was his own arm, set in a cast from hand to elbow, lying across his chest at a right angle. He blinked a few more times until he could distinguish the person dressed in white from the bright light behind him. He did not know why he suddenly thought of the girl and boy in the park and the Basiji guards who were interrogating them. He heard water being poured into a glass. There was an IV attached to his right arm. The person dressed in a white frock bent over him and again held his eye wide open and shined a bright light in it. The nurse raised the head of his bed and helped him slowly drink some water. As if it were washing everything away, he started to breathe more easily. "Can I smoke a cigarette?"

The scent of the nurse's perfume, infused with the smell of rubbing alcohol, made him feel nauseated. "May I have some more water?"

The nurse filled the glass again. "You don't have any pain, do you?"

She had delicate hands, but a large nose.

"No."

She helped him drink. "Can you lift the arm with the IV in it?"

He raised his arm.

"If you start feeling pain, ring the buzzer above your head."

She went over to the bed across the room and started reading the chart of a patient in a full body cast. His face was bandaged, and he had one arm and one leg in traction. The nurse asked, "Are you in pain?"

The patient slowly moved his hand, which had an IV in it, from side to side. The nurse put the chart back in its place and walked out of the room.

Kamran looked down at his legs under the blanket. He moved his toes, bent his knees, and pushed away the blanket. He heard what sounded like a moan. He looked up. The patient across the room was wiggling his fingers and quietly groaning. He ignored him and tried to sit up. The man's groans grew louder and his fingers started to wiggle faster. Kamran looked up at the buzzer. He slowly raised his torso and, cursing the big-nosed nurse under his breath, pressed the buzzer.

"Are you in pain?" the nurse asked as she walked in.

He wished he could lift his thousand-kilo cast and pound it on her head.

"This guy doesn't seem to be doing too well." He turned his gaze toward the patient who had now quieted down. "Just before you came in, he was moaning and twitching around."

The nurse reluctantly looked over at the other patient. "He's fine. He's been here for a month. He puts on the same show every time there's someone new in the room. Don't worry. Do you need anything?"

"No, I just want to know who brought me to the hospital."

The nurse raised her eyebrows and said, "I don't know. You were brought in during the morning shift. When I got here in the afternoon, your wife was here. She went home, but she'll be back soon. Don't worry."

When the nurse left, he thought about his "wife" and the blue outfit she was wearing.

An old man walked into the room. As soon as he saw Kamran, he said, "So, you're finally conscious."

He went over to the other patient and said, "Do you need anything, son?"

Kamran saw the patient move his fingers and heard him moan. The old man walked back to Kamran and asked, "Are you okay?"

"I'm fine, thanks."

"You were unconscious when they brought you in. The doctor said it's nothing serious. He took an x-ray of your head and checked."

"Thanks. Is he your son?"

The old man leaned forward and turned his ear to him. "What?"

"Is he your son?" he asked louder.

The old man sighed and looked at the heap of plaster and bandages. "My son. Yes, he's my son. He's been here for an entire month."

"Was he in an accident?" he said, louder this time.

"Huh?"

Kamran regretted his question and simply smiled. He decided to keep quiet and avoid having to repeat everything. The old man went and stood next to his son's bed. "He was as handsome as could be." He looked at Kamran. "Thank God, you're not hurt too badly. You'll go home today. And I have to bear my own pain. Still, I thank God." He looked up at the ceiling. "But there's one thing I don't understand. What will and wisdom was at work for such a disaster to happen to us. What uncommitted sin are we paying for? This kid didn't pray, he was wayward, true. But he was just young and foolish." His son's fingers twitched, and he moaned loudly. "All-forgiving, compassionate God, you should have had mercy on his youth. Still, thank God, thank God."

The young man's fingers moved again and this time he groaned even louder, like someone who wanted to shout, but a hand was gagging him. The old man caressed his face and said, "It's all right, son. You'll get better."

He turned to Kamran and smiled. "He'll be fine. I pray for him every day. He's a good boy. I remember the day he came and said, 'Dad, I want a motorcycle. One of those big ones.' He wasn't harsh with me at all. He was so polite…"

The youth's fingers were now moving alarmingly fast. But, oblivious to this, the old man carried on. "...I never denied anything to anyone, not even to strangers, lest I hurt their feelings. How could I deny my own son? I had some inheritance here and there from my father, God rest his soul. It was mostly land and property. As God is my witness, all I cared about were my children and the tough times they had to live through, otherwise..."

The old man's eyes turned to the door that had just opened. The girl walked in. "Indeed, she's a good wife," he said. "Cherish her. She sat with you from the moment they brought you in."

"Who's going to hear you, dear father?" the girl said.

The old man cupped his hand behind his ear. "What did you say, my girl?"

The girl put the single stem of white flower she was holding at the foot of the bed, walked over to the old man, and said, "I asked if your son is feeling better."

"No, my girl, what better? But I'm content if God is content." He blew his nose in a handkerchief. "I was telling you... I swear to the God who..."

The girl picked up the glass and the water pitcher and quietly said, "Oh no, here he goes again, babbling nonstop. Is he telling you the story of the wayward son and his motorcycle?" She smiled at the old man.

"Yes."

"If you let him, he'll drive you crazy, rattling on and on until tomorrow morning. I'll go and get more water."

He was becoming bored. He smiled at the old man and, ignoring what he was saying, tried to slide the flower up with his toes. The girl came back and put the stem in the half-filled glass.

"I was sure you would wake up. The doctor was worried that your head may have taken a nasty blow." She leaned forward. "I didn't tell him that your head didn't work right to begin with and that hopefully it has now had some sense knocked into it. I told everyone I'm your wife. Make sure you don't give me away. And I gave my consent and let the guy who knocked you upside down off the hook. The poor thing is young, and so handsome. I felt sorry for him. In any case, you're not the type to want to give him a hard time."

"You're the one who brought me to the hospital?"

"No, your dear auntie showed up like a saving angel, grabbed you by the tail, and brought you here. Are you always this scatterbrained when you cross the street?"

"Are you in a romantic mood, bringing me a flower?"

"I plucked it from the hospital garden," she said, laughing. "The security guard rushed over, but I gave him a smile that'll keep him turned on all night."

He looked over at the old man. "Be polite, at least here."

"Don't worry, he's a big flirt! The old chatterbox was sweet-talking me this morning."

She laughed out loud. The old man smiled and said, "God bless you, God bless you for loving your man so much." He turned to Kamran. "You got lucky. In this day and age, a good wife is like the elixir of life. Value her. This poor boy…" He pulled the sheet higher up on his son. "He had no luck. And then that wife of his…"

"Let him carry on as long as he wants," the girl said. "Are you in any pain?"

The old man was still talking.

"I feel sorry for him."

"You should feel sorry for us, getting stuck with someone even more miserable than we are."

He wanted to shift his broken arm. The girl gave him a hand, and then she sat at the foot of the bed with her back to the old man, who was still talking.

"Does it hurt?"

"You're just like that big-nosed nurse, constantly asking the same question."

"The hell with you. You're comparing me and my delicate nose to that ugly hag?" She got up from the bed. "The doctor said you can go home. There's nothing the hell wrong with you other than a broken arm. I'll go settle the bill."

When the girl left, he suddenly remembered the ball sitting motionless in the corner of the balcony in the brick building. He thought about the boy and his sleepy mother's unkempt hair when she came out, scolded him, and dragged him back inside.

———————————

He opened his eyes and saw the rays of sun shining in through the gap in the curtain. He blinked and squinted his eyes. He pushed the weight of the cast to the other side and turned his back to the window. His bladder was full. He contracted his stomach muscles, bent his knees, and massaged his back. The pressure on his bladder forced him to again straighten his legs. He stretched his body and got up. His broken arm itched right above his wrist. He stuck his finger under the cast as far as it would go and scratched his forearm. Then he went to the window and looked out at the second-floor balcony of the brick building. When he had made sure that the ball was still there, he went into the bathroom and peed with pleasure.

Still crouching over the squat toilet, he tilted forward to stretch his lower back even more. He leaned his broken arm on the water spigot and remembered the previous day's predicament of washing himself. He had been forced to put a bowl next to the faucet, fill it with water, and take one handful of water at a time to clean himself. By the time he had walked out of the bathroom, the cast on his arm was half-soaked. The girl had laughed and said, "You could have used your other hand, silly."

She had gone to the kitchen, returned with a large pot, and taken it to the bathroom.

"A pot won't do."

"Oh, I couldn't find anything more appropriate among your wide selection of kitchenware."

She had given him a big, noisy kiss on the cheek.

"And this is your bye-bye kiss. All romantic."

The brown lipstick she had carefully put on before they left the hospital, while the old man stood ogling her, must have smeared on his cheek.

He had intently said, "Stay."

"I get bored quickly if I stay in one place for too long. And I have to earn a living one way or another."

She had slung her black handbag over her shoulder.

"But you don't have money troubles."

"It all belongs to my mother who's getting remarried. I get nothing."

"Why? Didn't your father leave anything for you in his will?"

"The poor man didn't have a penny to his name. Is the interrogation over?"

"So it's all about money?"

"You're starting to bore me."

He grabbed the girl by the arm and dragged her to the closet. "Here, perhaps you won't be so bored now."

He took the duffel bag out, emptied the wads of thousand-toman bills and his clothes onto the floor, and pulled out the stacks of dollar bills. The girl chuckled and opened her eyes wide. "Wow! You're in good shape."

"For you."

He stuffed the money in the girl's handbag.

"And what do I have to do in exchange? Chain myself to you?" She took the money out of her handbag and put it on the table. "I'm leaving."

"As a matter of fact," he said. "I'm leaving, too."

"And going where?"

"Maybe I'll buy a car and hit the road."

"And then what?"

"If I knew, I wouldn't be going."

The girl took a cigarette from the pack on the table and said, "And, of course, you will drive off into the sunset, just like in the movies, right?" She laughed and lit the cigarette.

"I slept through sunrise all the time, maybe sunset is a better match for me."

"I like the sun to set in the middle of a trip. If it's at the start of the trip, I get depressed, and it's worse if it sets at the end. And sunrise drives me nuts. It belongs to thinkers, to those who want to get somewhere in life, and to those who have to leave home at the crack of dawn to earn a miserable bite of bread."

"Or to those who have the tenacity to call and wake someone up, so that he can watch the sun rise and think that he is supposedly happy and enjoying his freedom. Right? Now, which one of them is more ridiculous?"

The girl stood up. "Well, enough games. It was nice, lovely…" She kissed him on the cheeks and started to leave.

"Take the money. It's of no use to me anymore. I'm not kidding."

"If you had shaved off that beard, I would have stayed long enough for another five or six big kisses. Tell the ants I said goodbye. I don't speak their language."

When the door closed behind her, he looked over at the ants, at the closet door that remained open, and at the clothes and odds and ends strewn on the living room floor. He got up, rubbed his back, carefully raised his broken arm, and with his other hand pulled up his pants. He stood in front of the mirror and made faces at himself. He brushed his teeth, combed his hair with his fingers, and tried not to look at his beard.

He went to the kitchen, drank a glass of cold milk, and, without changing into his exercise clothes, left the apartment. He strolled to the park without counting his steps. He drank at the water fountain and walked two laps around the park. He stretched with one arm. On his way back, he did not stop at the bakery. He bought a razor from the shop next door to it and slowly jogged the rest of the way home. When he opened the building's front door, the usual stench seemed stronger to him. Hashemzadeh was standing on the landing between the ground floor and the first floor, making wisecracks at the landlady's brother and complaining about the foul smell. The old woman who came every other day to mop the staircase was standing on the steps between them, holding her bucket and waiting. Wearing a pair of striped pajama pants and a black vest, the landlady's brother was standing with his hands on the doorframe, gaping at her. Kamran tried not to look at Hashemzadeh. He was not in the mood to listen to him carry on and make a fuss. Hashemzadeh looked at his broken arm and shook his head. As he passed the first floor, he caught a glimpse of Hashemzadeh's wife peeking through the door. She quickly moved back, but he felt her eyes following him. Then he heard her say out loud, "Let it go. Come on up. It's not the poor old man's fault."

He closed the door and went straight to the bathroom. He had just started shaving off his beard when the telephone rang. He ignored it. In tandem with the rings, he cut his chin in two places. Blood leaked into the white foam. He wiped it away and shaved under his chin.

He went and sat at the kitchen table and waited for the kettle to boil. He wished he could just then dive into deep waters and swim all the way to the bottom. A fly sat on the table, near the invisible stain he had wiped clean a few days earlier. With a whisk of his hand, he caught it. He opened his fist slightly and felt the fly struggling to set itself free. With the thumb and index finger of his other hand, he pulled off one of its wings and put the fly back on the table for it to fly away on a single wing. Smiling, he took a dollop of jam for the ants and put it on their tray. He went back to the kitchen, picked up the fly's torn-off wing with his fingertips, then stuck it in the jam. And he continued to stare at the fly thrashing about.

PART III

IN STEP

He shifted his broken arm on the soft flesh of his thigh and held the steering wheel with his fingertips. With his other hand, he put the cup next to the handbrake and poured himself some tea from the flask. As he drove along the bumpy road, he could hear something clanking in the back of the car. It sounded like there was something under the back seat. He had to remember to look down there the first chance he got. He wedged the cup between his legs, so that he could hold the steering wheel with his good hand while waiting for the tea to cool a little.

When he drove around the next bend, he again switched hands, sipped on the tea without any sugar, and lit a cigarette. After he took the last puff, he pulled over and stopped on the shoulder of the road. He looked around. He saw nothing but oak trees, boulders, a cliff, and the valley below.

He got out of the car and opened the back door. He leaned down and looked under the back seat. There was nothing there. He climbed back behind the wheel and drove off. The clanking started again and did not allow him to think about anything else. The last cigarette had left an acrid taste in his mouth. He scraped the ends of his upper teeth over his tongue. He felt there was still a bitter film in the back of his mouth. He scraped it with his fingernail, rolled down the window, and spat out.

He inhaled the crisp morning air deep into his lungs and closed his eyes. He did not look at the road. He pushed down on the gas pedal to let the cool air blow against his face, to allow every cell in his skin to absorb that deep and unexpected pleasure, and to feel free and light and closer to the distant darkness behind his eyelids... if only he could block out the clanking that had now blended with the sound of bleating and bells, which was growing louder and more rapid by the second. He opened his eyes and saw a herd of sheep up ahead. He was speeding toward them. He clutched the wheel and tried to steer the car to the right and back onto the asphalt. He started tapping on the brake, trying to slow down. The car skidded to the left. All he knew was that he was hurled up and down, and his head hit the roof a few times. He ran his hand over his face and touched the side of his forehead that had slammed into the side window.

He climbed out of the car. He had crashed into an oak tree on the side of the road. He turned and looked at the old man standing over the bodies of three sheep and beating himself on the head with both hands. A ten- or twelve-year-old boy was chasing after the scattered herd, trying to gather them. The old man looked at him for a moment and then went over to his donkey and pulled out a knife from his rug saddlebag. He walked back to one of the lifeless sheep, cut off its head, and sat down on the ground next to it and started shouting and hollering. The other two sheep had already died and were haram, unfit to eat, but he had managed to slaughter the third one while it was still alive, so that its meat would be halal. Kamran had seen many similar accidents in that region where stockbreeding was prevalent. Often, the shepherds had no choice but to move their herds across roads. The boy left the sheep roaming among the bushes and trees alongside the road and went over to the old man. Then he looked at him and his car.

His left shoulder ached. He took off the sling suspending his broken arm from his neck, and flexed and massaged his shoulder. The boy was dragging the dead sheep off the road. The old man wiped his bloody knife on the wool of the ewe he had slaughtered and went over to the boy, took the dead sheep from him, and let them drop back down on the asphalt. "But they're in the way," the boy said. "Let me move them off the road."

The old man shook his head, mumbled something, and did not allow the boy to touch the sheep again. "Don't worry," the boy said. "I'll make him pay for them." Then he brought his goatskin water bag and poured water for the old man to wash his hands. There were black blood clots on the asphalt as far as the white divider line in the middle of the road.

Kamran went and stood over the ewe the old man had slaughtered. It was larger than the other two. The old man had probably not allowed the boy to move the cadavers off the road until they had settled on damages and restitution. He heard a car honking behind him. It sped by and honked a few more times.

"Tell your father not to worry. I'll pay for the sheep."

"He's not my father. He's my uncle."

"The sheep belong to him?"

"Fifty are ours, fifty are his."

He turned to the old man. "How much should I pay you for the sheep? What are they worth?"

The old man said nothing. The boy quietly said, "He's mute. He can't speak."

"Mute?"

The old man was struggling to bring back the sheep that had wandered off.

"Ask him how much he wants for them."

He went back to his car. The left headlight was broken and there was a dent above the left front tire. He opened the hood and checked the radiator and the belt. Then he turned the engine on and off. The front fender was badly damaged on the left side and it had broken loose. He took four stacks of thousand-toman bills from the duffel bag in the trunk and put one of them in his pocket. He walked over to the old man, who was now sitting next to a hollowed and charred tree trunk, filling a black kettle from the goatskin water bag. The boy was adding dry twigs to the larger branches stacked under the kettle. The old man eyed the money he was holding and struck a match. The boy took a bundle from the rug saddlebag on the donkey and said, "Have you had breakfast, sir?"

"No."

"Uncle said I should brew some tea for you."

Kamran sat down on a thick root that had grown above the ground and said, "Did you ask him about the price of the sheep?" He put the money in front of the old man. "If it's not enough, I'll give you more."

He smiled at the old man. The old man did not smile back. He made a few incomprehensible sounds and motioned for the boy to explain what he was trying to say.

"This is too much, sir," the boy said. "They weren't worth this much."

The old man took one of the stacks and started counting the bills. The boy opened the bundle and said, "It's local butter and bread. Help yourself."

The old man put a few of the thousand-toman bills that he had separated on the ground in front of Kamran and tucked the rest of the money in his pocket. He gestured to the boy again, said something, and pointed to the sheep that the sun was now shining on. "He says the ewe he slaughtered is yours. It's *halal*."

The old man went and dragged the other two sheep off the road and into a ditch, then began covering them with rocks.

"He's burying them," the boy said. "Eat some breakfast."

Kamran put a piece of bread and butter in his mouth and asked, "Don't you go to school?"

"What good is school?" the boy said as he took a handful of tea leaves from a plastic bag and put them in the kettle. "I want to go to the village, to my sister's husband. He works for the Department. They pay thirty or forty a month. And my sister works in the Watershed Management Camp. She says, 'Come here. The engineer is a nice man. I'll ask him to give you work.'"

"What does she do there?"

"My sister sweeps the camp and cooks for the engineer. Her husband is a watch guard."

The boy poured some tea in a dented metal cup and put it in front of him. "Please." Then he took the plastic lid off a small bowl of sugar cubes and put it next to the cup.

"What is your brother-in-law's name?"

"He's my uncle's son," the boy said, pointing to the old man. "His name is Ali-Sina. He says the engineer really likes him. He says he'll ask him to put me to work on the check dams. Do you know what check dams are?"

The heat of the cup burned his fingers. The breeze scattered the bills on the dirt. The boy quickly gathered them and weighed them down with a stone.

"Do you know how to count?"

"I went to school up to fourth grade. You think I can't count?"

He took the bills and handed them to the boy. "Let me see you count."

The old man was still piling rocks on top of the ditch. Kamran waved to him and smiled. The old man waved back but did not smile. The boy said, "There are thirty."

He looked at the boy with the remnants of the smile still on his face. "If you can convince your uncle to skin and gut that sheep right here…" He pointed to the tree branch above his head. "… I'll give him the thirty thousand tomans, as well."

The boy's eyes sparkled. "Thirty thousand tomans? Do you think I'm a cripple? I'll hang it myself, right here. Don't you worry."

The boy hurried over to the donkey and returned with a rope. The tea was now cooler and he could hold the cup. The old man stomped on the rocks a few times, as if trying to set them, then walked over to the boy, and mumbled and signaled something to him.

He took a sip of tea to wash down a large piece of bread and butter, and watched the old man and the boy. He was reaching for the kettle to refill his cup when his cell phone started to ring. Startled, the old man turned toward him. The boy took the old man's chin, turned his head back toward himself, and mimicked the act of cutting.

The caller's telephone number had not registered on the screen. Kamran took his cup and a couple of sugar cubes and walked a few steps away from the tree. He put on his earphones and wondered who could be calling him at that hour of the morning—it was not even 7:00 yet.

"Hello?"

"Hey, are you awake? The sun rose a long time ago."

He took a sip of his tea and walked farther away from the tree. "Hi."

"I miss you."

"Sure you do!"

"Honestly. Believe me."

"I believe you. And?"

"I was worried about you."

"You? Worried about me?"

"Will it do any good if I finish every sentence with 'Believe me'? How's your arm? Still in a cast?"

The boy had hung the sheep from the tree and the old man was walking toward it with a knife.

"You didn't sign my cast so that I would think of you every time I look at it. Is your mother still around? Did she marry that fatso?"

"Which one do you mean? The one with a moustache or the bald one?"

"No matter which one, she still has better taste than you who go after bearded guys and then leave them hanging. At least your mother knows what she wants."

"Actually, that's why I called."

The old man was deftly skinning the sheep, while the boy, carrying a tub, was walking down the hill toward the low valley.

Kamran was strolling near the ditch where the sheep were buried. He kicked a piece of wood that looked like a segment of a root. It was twisted and curved, and there were regular arched lines running along its length, from thick to thin and merging together. The root landed next to the rocks covering the sheep.

"I know you shaved off that beard. You look gorgeous. I thought we should get together so that I can kiss you a few times. I'm pining for you. Can you believe it?"

"Who told you I shaved off my beard?"

He sat next to the ditch, put his cup on a flat stone, and hit the piece of wood against a rock to shake off the dirt.

"What's that noise?"

"Do you know the prayer for the dead?"

The girl's hysterical laugh blended with the sound of the wood hitting against the rock.

"Have you ever gone to someone's graveside?"

The sun peeking above the snow-covered mountains blinded him and did not let him see what the old man did with the sheep's intestines, which he had grabbed onto like a piece of rope and pulled out hand over hand. He turned slightly away from the sun and held up the piece of wood so that light would shine on its darker side, which had probably been buried in the ground for many years. The boy returned from the valley with the tub filled with water.

"Do you know where I am right now? At the graveside of two sheep."

"How fortunate!"

"For who? For the sheep or for me? I'm trying to remember the last time I recited the prayer for the dead over someone's grave."

"If I knew the prayer, I would say it for my dad. It's his own fault, he never taught it to me. Do you think I'm a bad person?"

"Now I remember. I was twelve. Shall I tell you what happened?"

"You didn't answer my question."

"I was watching the crowd praying over my grandmother's coffin. Her body was wrapped in a white shroud, in an open coffin. They were standing there, praying, and my father started signaling to me with his eyes. I couldn't understand what he was trying to say. As the crowd genuflected in prayer, he grabbed my arm, pulled me to his side, and motioned that I should genuflect, too. I was thinking, how are we supposed to prostrate on the dirt?"

"If you ask me, you should donate the halal sheep to the needy. They say it brings good fortune."

He set the piece of wood on an elevated rock so that its dark, wet side faced the sun.

"What are you up to, girl? What are you after?"

She laughed and said, "But you know everything about me, you idiot!"

The old man was washing his hands. The boy was walking toward him.

"You're the idiot, not me. Where are you now?"

The arched lines on the piece of wood were gleaming in the sun. He got up. "Hello?... Hello?... Hello?"

He said the third "hello" in a louder voice. The old man turned and looked at him, his hand remaining motionless on the sheep's rolled up skin.

"We skinned and gutted the sheep," the boy said. "What shall we do with it?"

He looked at the cell phone screen. The line had not disconnected. He nodded toward his car and said, "Take it over there."

He picked up the piece of wood.

"Who was that?"

"Why the heck did you stop talking?"

"Was it a woman? She sounded strange."

"But you already know everything, Madam Soothsayer, heavenly shrew. Do you want me to talk to you like this?"

"Why are you always looking for a meaning behind everything? Maybe everything is as easy and as simple as it appears. Is it necessary to constantly search for an underlying reason?"

"Do you know what I would do to you if you were here?"

She laughed. "It would have been great to spend some cozy time together right there under the tree you crashed your car into. And then we could smoke a whole pack of cigarettes and blow the smoke up in the air. Come on, wouldn't it have been just perfect?"

"I don't know why I can't get angry at you."

The dampness of the piece of wood had cooled the palm of his hand. He thought if he cleaned and varnished it properly, if he patiently worked on it, he could use it as a decorative piece in the living room. He was certain Fariba would say, *Again you found some rubbish in the boondocks and brought it home?*

The old man had thrown the sheep up on his shoulder and was carrying it to the car. He heard a loud smack on the phone.

"What was that?"

"A kiss. I wanted it to be nice and juicy, now that you've shaved off your beard. Bye!"

"Hey!... Hello?"

He looked at the screen and called the girl a few more times. He went and put the piece of wood in the car, in front of the passenger seat. Then he opened the trunk, pushed his duffel bag and the gasoline tank to the side, and motioned for the old man to put the sheep in there.

The boy spread the sheepskin on the bottom of the trunk and rolled out its legs, then the old man laid the carcass on top of it. The boy handed Kamran a plastic bag and said, "Here's its heart and liver." Kamran put the bag next to the piece of wood in front of the passenger seat.

He lit a cigarette and examined the front fender again. Then he shook hands with the old man and, speaking loudly, said, "Are you satisfied, father?"

"Sure, why wouldn't he be satisfied?" the boy replied. "He got his money."

Kamran was about to blurt out, *Say hello to Tajmah.* He checked himself and said, "Say hello to your family."

Surprised, the boy stared at him and laughed. The old man frowned at the boy and pointed to the sheep.

———————————

In the rearview mirror, he saw the old man and the boy cross the road. He slowed down, poured a little tea from the flask into the cup, swirled it around, and emptied it out the window. He was holding the steering wheel with his left hand, his broken arm and shoulder were throbbing. He filled the cup halfway with tea, took repeated puffs on his half-finished cigarette, and held the smoke in his lungs for a long time. He tossed the cigarette butt out the window. A bus behind him honked several times and sped by. He pushed down on the gas pedal. The fender rattled more loudly. As he drank his tea, he listened to the noise coming from the back seat. It was becoming too annoying to ignore. He wondered what it was about the noise that bothered him so much. Was it the fact that he did not know what was causing it, or was it the noise itself? It sounded like an empty soda can rolling around on a metal surface as the car went uphill and downhill. He slammed on the brakes. For an instant the noise grew sharper and then it stopped. A few kilometers ahead, past a natural spring on the side of the road, it started again, oscillating like the grating of a cradle's dry hinges.

He pulled over onto the dirt shoulder and drove up to a roadside hut built with oak branches and sitting on a cement platform. The bus that had honked for him was on the other side of the road, and its passengers were getting off. If Fariba were there, she would have said, *I don't like crowds*. And she would not have looked at the towering, moss-covered boulder with the gentle current of a wide waterfall cascading down its uneven surface, sinking into a bed of short, green weeds, and resurfacing farther away, clear and cold.

With one foot out of the car, he stood up and shouted at the young tanned man carrying a kettle to the waterfall. "Do you have the setup for kebab?"

"Please come. You are always welcome here."

He looked at the hut. The young man was smiling and walking over to him. "Please come."

He shook the young man's hand and said, "Do I know you?"

"Don't you remember, Engineer? You gave me a ride a few months ago. I'd brought a Turkish scarf for my betrothed."

Kamran laughed and took out his pack of cigarettes. "You're in good shape, thank God! You're looking pretty fit. Is your military service over?" He reached into the car and took out the plastic bag with the sheep's liver and heart.

"Rah!" the young man exclaimed, waving his arms in the air. "Service is over. And I got married and got it over with."

Something hit the rear windshield. He looked back and saw a small boy running after his ball, which was rolling into the wet weeds on the other side of the car. The boy's mother was franticly chasing him. "Don't go in the mud!"

He handed the plastic bag to the young man. "Do you have a fire going? I'm in a bit of a hurry."

"Of course. Shall I grill all of it?"

"Three skewers would be enough."

The young man walked over to the hut and shouted at his helper, who had gone and filled the kettle, "Get a move on, boy, stop dragging your heels! Can't you see we have work to do?"

The small boy with the ball was ankle-deep in water, and his mother was pulling his arm to stop him from going in any deeper. "Your pants and shoes are soaking wet! Stop right there." She turned to a man who was fiddling with the engine of a charcoal grey Peugeot Persia parked near the hut. "Youssef, come fetch his ball for him. He is covered with mud."

The boy yanked his arm away and said, "I can get it myself."

With his head still under the hood, the man yelled, "Can't you see I'm busy?"

One of the bus passengers, who was standing on a rock nearby, said, "Lady, this place is all algae and silt. We have to drag the ball over with a stick or something." And he looked around, probably searching for a stick.

Kamran lit another cigarette and, ignoring that his shoes and pants were getting wet, walked along the edge of the weeds to the moss-covered boulder. He sat on a thick root that had surfaced from the shallow water and took off his shoes and socks, rolled up his pants, and let the weeds coil and wave around his ankles. The man who was standing on a rock had found a branch and was trying to push the ball toward the woman. The passengers of the bus were wandering around the hut. One of them had gone over to the woman's husband and was peeking under the hood of his car. The boy was still struggling to free himself from his mother's grip. A middle-aged man was leaning against the loose fender of his car, ogling the woman. Her headscarf had slid off her hair, and every time she leaned forward, the curve of her behind became more prominent under her coverall.

He flicked his cigarette ash on the dancing weeds, so that he could hear the short sizzling sound it made as it hit the water. He leaned back against the wet tree trunk and, through its branches and leaves, looked up at the boulder and the glistening moss. He ignored the short scream that probably came from the woman. He closed his eyes and let the water's refreshing chill travel from the soles of his feet to every cell in his body. He listened to the water trickle and the leaves rustle, waiting for the commotion of the people around him to fade away, so that he would hear nothing but the birds chirping. They seemed to be constantly talking and not getting tired of all that tweeting and twittering. Remembering his childhood wish—to be able to speak the language of birds and to understand what they said to each other when they gathered in the mornings and late afternoons, and fluttered and sprang around—made him want to laugh.

"Mr. Engineer." The young man was standing at the edge of the weeds, holding a tray. "Shall I bring it over to you, or will you come to the hut?"

He went and took the tray from him. "Thanks a lot. Tell your helper to fill the flask of tea in my car."

"Sure. I'll take care of it myself."

The man closed the hood of his car and put their tea basket in the trunk. Then he turned to the woman chasing after the boy and shouted, "Hurry up, missus!"

Kamran set the tray on his lap, pushed the bread aside, and started eating the chunks of grilled liver.

He held a few sprigs of basil up to his nose, drew in their scent, and ate them all in one mouthful. He ate a few more pieces of liver one after the other and watched the woman, who was now carrying the boy to the car while trying to pull her headscarf back over her hair. The boy clawed at her dyed, frizzy hair. When she bent down in pain, he escaped her arms and cried, "I want to play! I'm not coming. I want my ball."

The woman looked over at the passengers of the bus and tidied her scarf. The man ran after the boy, scolding him. The sound of Kamran's cell phone ringing mingled with the shouts of the father and son. He looked at the screen, wiped his fingers on the bread, and answered it.

"Hello?"

"Hi, Kami."

"Hi."

"Where are you? Have you left yet?"

He put the tray to the side and lifted his feet out of the water.

"Yes, dear. I'm on my way."

The boy was standing in the middle of the weeds and splashing silt and algae at his father, who was taking off his shoes and rolling up his pants.

"I've been trying to reach you since this morning. It either says you're not available or it doesn't ring at all."

"It's all thanks to the Minister of Telecommunications. What's the guy's name?"

"Stop joking. Where are you now?"

"I stopped at the spring. Do you know which one I mean?"

"The one below that mountain pass? I always forget its name. The one with all the twists and turns."

"The spring with a small hut next to it, where the buses stop. Don't you remember?"

The boy was running away from his father when he slipped and fell in the weeds and was covered with mud from head to toe. His father tucked him under his arm, picked up his shoes with his free hand, and walked barefoot back to his car.

"Mom wants to know what you'd like for lunch. Is fresh herb stew okay?"

"Yes, that's fine."

"Will you be here by noon?"

"I'll be there, give or take an hour."

"Be careful. Drive slow, alright?"

The boy was clutching his ball as his mother changed his clothes. The man was washing his feet.

"Yes, dear. Say hello to your mom and dad."

"Mom says hello, too. We're waiting. By the way…"

There were a few seconds of silence.

"What is it?"

"Nothing. I'll tell you when you get here. It's just that there's something missing from my things. And I can't ask Nakissa about it."

He remembered the small rock, the gift for their first wedding anniversary. "If you mean the broom and dustpan, I gave them to Sima."

"Oh, you… wait till you get here. I know what to do with you. You took it?"

"The Afghan guy that Kamali brought over to clean the house was so slow, and the truck driver kept nagging that he wanted to get on the road as soon as possible. It was all such a mess that I forgot the broom and dustpan."

"Fine, whatever you say. Keep teasing me. I'll show you when you get here. I will look through my things one more time. You better pray I find the rock."

"I always pray. Say hello to everyone."

He disconnected the line, took the flask of tea from the young man, and said, "Keep the rest of the liver and heart. I'm traveling and they'll go bad in the car."

"Travel safe. Visit us when you come back."

He took a deep puff on his cigarette and looked over at the boy and his frustrated mother. She was taking a pair of slippers to the man, who was waiting with his feet propped up on a rock. She tossed the slippers in front of him. The boy was bouncing his ball against a tree and catching it.

He continued to watch the boy and his colorful ball, which was now rolling into the weeds, until he reached the turn in the road. He drove around the bend and did not see which direction the ball had gone. His stomach was upset. He thought it was perhaps because of the local butter and the liver and basil he had stuffed himself with, or the countless cigarettes he had chain-smoked since that morning. He ignored the clanking under the back seat and lit another cigarette. He smelled gasoline. He sniffed again and burped. The taste of liver and basil rose from his stomach to his mouth and mixed with the smell of gasoline. He felt queasy. He tossed the cigarette out the window and craved a cold soda. He could drive back to the hut and drink one with his feet soaking in the numbingly cold pool at the foot of the waterfall. But that was too much bother. The next pass was not far and he could stop at the coffeehouse down the mountain from it. There, he could also buy a couple of blocks of ice to put around the carcass in the trunk. Near the pass, he reduced his speed and got behind a line of cars that had slowed down. He turned off the air conditioner and rolled down the window. There was a police car at the head of the pass, and an officer was urging the drivers who were stopping to drive on. The driver of the car in front of him called out, "Officer, was there an accident?"

"Move along, sir. Don't stop."

A man standing by the side of the road said, "A Pride drove off the cliff and burst into flames. They say there was one person in it."

The driver shook his head and drove off. Kamran tried to peer down the cliff, hoping to see the valley floor. Farther ahead, he saw a short skid mark on the asphalt. A few people were leaning over a boulder, looking down. As he drove down the mountain and around the twists and turns, the burned car and the crowd gathered around it kept coming into view and disappearing again. He thought the smell of gasoline had become stronger. When he parked in front of the coffeehouse, he opened the hood and checked the engine. Then he examined the cap on the gas tank and realized that the smell was coming from the trunk. He remembered the container of gasoline. When he opened the trunk, the pungent smell of gasoline and stale meat wafted out. The container had fallen on its side and was leaking onto the sheepskin. A narrow stream had trickled under the carcass and his duffel bag. He picked up the container and tightened its plastic cap. Then he took the duffel bag, checked his clothes, smelled them, and took them out and spread them under the sun. The sheep's carcass smelled of rancid meat mixed with blood and gasoline. He spread a few sheets of newspaper in the trunk. When he was sure there was no gasoline left on the bottom, he checked the container again and lodged it at the far end of the trunk so that it would not move.

He closed the trunk and went into the coffeehouse. He bought a can of soda and gulped it down in one breath. The smell of kebab made him feel sick. One of the customers was telling the proprietor about the Pride that had plunged down the cliff and its driver who had burned to a crisp. He went back outside and gathered his clothes. As he went to put the duffel bag on the floor in front of the back seat, he saw a crumpled soda can under the front passenger seat and remembered the clanking. He took the can and tossed it out. As he got back into the car, he saw a charcoal grey Peugeot Persia drive by. The boy he had seen at the waterfall was rolling his ball back and forth behind the rear window.

He watched the boy until the Peugeot disappeared among the trees alongside the river in the valley. He remembered a ball sitting in the corner of an apartment balcony and a sleepy woman with scruffy hair. Before reaching the trees, he pulled over next to a low cliff and opened the trunk. With great difficulty, he dragged out the carcass with one hand and threw it among the boulders and trees below. As he drove off, he saw a drop of blood on his cast. He had to remember to thoroughly wash the trunk when he reached the river.

Photo: Renee Rosensteel

ABOUT THE AUTHOR

Yaghoub Yadali, a fiction writer from Iran, has directed for television and worked for *Roshd Magazine* as the editor of the film section. He is the author of the short story collections *Sketches in the Garden* (1997) and *Probability of Merriment and Mooning* (2001) and the novel *Rituals of Restlessness*, which won the 2004 Golshiri Foundation Award. His short stories, articles, and essays are published in Iran, Turkey, and the US. He has been writer-in-residence at the University of Iowa, Harvard University, and City of Asylum in Pittsburgh.

ABOUT THE TRANSLATOR

Sara Khalili is an editor and translator of contemporary Iranian literature. Her translations include *Censoring an Iranian Love Story* by Shahriar Mandanipour, *The Book of Fate* by Parinoush Saniee, *Kissing the Sword: A Prison Memoir* by Shahrnush Parsipur, and *Pomegranate Lady and Her Sons* by Goli Taraghi. She has also translated several volumes of poetry by Forough Farrokhzad, Simin Behbahani, Siavash Kasraii, and Fereydoon Moshiri. Her translations of Mandanipour's short stories have appeared in *The Literary Review, The Kenyon Review, The Virginia Quarterly Review, EPOCH,* Words without Borders, and PEN America. She lives in New York.